DREAMS AND SCHEMES

A HOPE HERRING COZY MYSTERY
BOOK 14

J. A. WHITING

NELL MCCARTHY

**To hear about new books and book sales, please sign up for my mailing list at:
jawhiting.com**

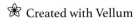 Created with Vellum

With thanks to our readers

Dream big

1

Hope Herring opened her umbrella and raised it over her head—not to ward off rain but to provide a bit of shade. It was the middle of the afternoon and the bleachers were too hot to sit on. Hope stood to one side, in her little circle of shade with perspiration forming on her forehead. She knew the heat index was well over a hundred and that made her wonder if the teams would even play. They were on the field, warming up so she assumed they intended to play. She thought that could be dangerous. Wouldn't it be better to postpone for a day or two, after the heat wave had dissipated? The least they could do would be to postpone the game till after dark. It would still be hot, but it wouldn't be so miserable. She glanced at the concession stand. Was it time for a lemonade or something else cool to drink?

The diamond cleared. The public address announcer went through the starting lineups for both teams. Soon, all the players and coaches were standing on the foul lines, scuffing dirt and spitting, just like their big-league counterparts. What was it about baseball that lent itself to decades-old traditions? Hope didn't know and at that moment, she didn't care. She just wanted to get out of the heat.

From behind the umpire, Hope's daughter Cori came out with the microphone in her hand. She marched to the pitcher's mound and stood on the rubber. She looked tiny compared to the college players. UNC-Wilmington was hosting a school Hope was not familiar with. Cori stood still as the announcer asked everyone to rise and remove their hats. The teams responded immediately, as did the fans all around. People stood, hands over hearts, and waited.

The moment of truth.

Hope crossed her fingers and said a silent prayer. Cori had sung the National Anthem before crowds many times before. It was an easy gig, and most stadiums and fields loved to have someone do the singing. The singer didn't need to be particularly talented ... he or she just had to hit the right notes and know the lyrics.

The only problem was that the anthem itself was not easy to sing. It had too much range. Too many shower singers discovered that standing before a big crowd did strange things to the vocal chords. That was one reason why Norrie, Cori's coach, had encouraged her to do the anthem every chance she could find.

Cori put the mic close to her lips and hit that first note.

Perfect.

Hope smiled. Cori belted out the anthem with the correct volume, rhythm, and pitch. Some people in the crowd joined in the singing, but they were no competition for her. For two minutes or so, the fans and teams were united as one.

Then, it all stopped.

Cori smiled and waved as the crowd applauded with enthusiasm.

The teams broke apart. One team ran out on the field, and the other filled the dugout and started gearing up for the plate. Traditions had been met. The game could begin. Hope nodded and waited.

"How was I?" Cori asked, as she appeared at Hope's side.

"How do you think you were?" Hope answered.

"I thought I nailed it, although the sound system here sucks." She pulled her long brown hair into a ponytail.

"Indeed, it does, and you're right, you did nail it. Getting used to singing the anthem?"

"If you sing it enough times, then there's nothing to fear."

"Exactly. So, what do you want to do now? I doubt you want to hang around and watch the game in this heat."

"Let's go someplace cool. It's really too hot out here."

"I agree. How about a movie? Is there something you want to see?"

Cori shook her head. "Nothing I've heard about, but I'll watch anything."

"Fair enough. Shall we go to Mayfair or the new cinema off seventeenth street."

"The new one."

"Sounds good to me. You do remember that school will be starting in a couple of weeks?"

"Don't remind me. I'm focused on the mall gig next Saturday."

"I just wanted you to be aware that the first day of school is coming fast."

The movie they chose was a romcom that was neither very romantic nor funny. Hope found her mind wandering, as she considered how she was going to ensure that Cori not only went to her voice lessons but also lived up to her gig commitments her manager was arranging. In the past, most of the work had been in Wilmington or Greenville, but Hope fully anticipated having to drive to Raleigh or Charlotte. Those weren't simple jaunts. She guessed there would be more overnight and weekend jobs coming up. That would put a strain on her finances because Cori would not be paid a lot of money. Hope shoved the worry out of her head and focused on the movie, which wasn't much of a story and was sort of a waste of time.

Just what Hope didn't need.

The movie was followed by pizza and the drive home. As Hope had come to expect, Cori wasn't very talkative. In the past, she and her daughter had enjoyed a lot of give-and-take. Cori was clever enough to engage Hope, to help her mother laugh. Moody wasn't what Hope had expected from her daughter.

"So, have you talked to Lottie lately?" Hope asked.

"My manager told me to be careful about friends.

She says that friends are never really friends. She says that if I become successful, my friends will resent me and do what they can to torpedo my career."

"True friends won't do that."

"It happens, Mom."

"You have to have people you trust around. You can't live without them. No person is an island. People need friends." Hope took a quick look at her daughter. "Your effort to become a singer is supposed to be fun."

Hope stared straight ahead, not at all sure she liked this new version of Cori. "Maybe singing isn't for you. I mean, if it makes you act against yourself, how satisfying can it be?

"I'm kidding, Mom," Cori said. "My manager really did say that stuff and I get what she means. If someone is successful, they can attract a lot of people who only want to be friends because you're famous. You have to be careful."

Hope thought for a moment. She didn't like what the manager was telling her daughter. The world had been divided into winners and losers. That wasn't the truth. There was a lot being thrown at the teen and Cori was going through that hormonal period where body and mind changed.

Hope remembered those years. They were trying at best. Teenagers had to navigate the seas of doubt, angst, and despair. It was never easy.

What could Hope do to help?

That was the real question. What could she do to ease the pressure, add some sunshine, help Cori sniff the flowers? The world could be a very happy place. How could Hope relay that to her daughter?

Cori said, "To tell you the truth, I sometimes don't know if my life is going up or down. I mean, I have a voice coach and a manager, and I sing in a lot of different venues, whenever I can. That's something. I don't have any friends in the music industry. No matter how they smile at me, I can't help but feel they want me to screw up somehow. You and I don't really know the rules about performing and singing and trying to get somewhere with it. I guess we'll just have to muddle through and learn as we go."

Hope reached over and took her daughter's hand. Sometimes, simple human touch was more important than thoughts and words. Hope didn't say anything, because Cori was right. They both wondered about the same things. Was their life on the up escalator or the down? Would tomorrow be a better day or a worse one? Were they pursuing the right goals? Were they planting seeds of joy or sorrow? How could they know?

Muddle through.

Cori was right. They would muddle through. They would wake up to each new day and do the best they could. Life didn't come with guarantees. It was take a swing and see if you hit one out of the park. It was all you could do.

"I read about these Chinese kids," Cori said. "They moved to this city that they named slacker city. It's where they lie flat. That means they don't do anything. Their motto is 'no buying a home, no car, no marriage, no baby, no consumption.' They don't want to do anything. They live in tents and eat two boxes of instant noodles a day. Most of their time is spent online, gaming and chatting and wasting time. They claim they have no future, so there's no reason to work. Better to lie down and exist online. I think we have our own slackers here. They take drugs, drink alcohol, and drift off into some kind stupor. I don't know. But, some of the kids in school feel like those Chinese kids. They think the world is going to burn to a crisp because of climate change. They don't believe they'll live as well as their parents. How can they?"

"What do you believe?"

Cori laughed out loud. "I try to believe as little as possible."

It was good to hear Cori laugh.

"And, I don't think it matters," Cori added.

"Why is that?"

"I think that life is like a battle. Every time you win a battle, another battle shows up to take its place. All that matters is winning the next battle but even that isn't so important because most of us are going to lose more than we win. That's just life. So, your real goal is just to put up a great fight. If you do that, if you really try, then you win in some sense. That sounds silly, doesn't it?"

"Not silly at all. In fact, it's a rather mature assessment of life. I happen to agree with you. I do think that what we call muddling through is exactly what you said—battling the best we can. I once read a statistic about Michael Jordan, perhaps the greatest basketball player of all time. It seems that he took the game-winning shot a lot. Why not, he was the best player out there. But he succeeded in winning the game rarely. He missed many more than he made. Did it matter? I don't think so. He did the best he could. It's the fight that's important."

Cori squeezed Hope's hand. "Thank you. I probably don't say that often enough, but I really am thankful that you're my mother. I'm happy, Mom. And I do care about my friends."

"You're welcome. Never forget that I love you, and I want you to find joy in your battles."

Cori laughed again. "The happy warriorette, that's me."

"That's us."

"Us and Max."

"Yes, we can't forget Max. I wonder what sort of predicament he's gotten himself into today."

"We'll soon know," Cori said with a smile as they drove into the driveway of their antique home.

When they'd moved from Ohio to North Carolina after the death of Hope's husband, the house had needed work, and over time, they'd been able to make a few updates. Hope had been nervous about the move. They hadn't known anyone in the state, but she'd needed a change so she accepted a teaching job in Castle Park and bought the house sight-unseen.

With its intricate woodwork and ornate details, the old Victorian home was a work of art. The paved walkway led to the wrap-around porch with beautifully carved columns and railings decorated with circular motifs.

Inside, there were high ceilings, beautiful hardwood floors, and the rooms were embellished with crown molding. In the dining room, tall windows let in natural light and a crystal chandelier hung overhead casting a warm, flickering glow across the room. The staircase with its carved banister led upstairs to the bedrooms, and a couple of marble fireplaces anchored the cozy sitting areas. Each room of the house was like a time capsule showcasing the fine craftmanship of yesteryear.

But what surprised Hope most about the house was that it came with a resident ghost, Maximillian Johnson.

As soon as Hope and Cori walked into the kitchen, their fluffy gray and white cat Bijou hurried over and rubbed their legs while they patted the feline.

In his forties when he was murdered, Max sat at the table dressed in a black robe, complete with cowl. If he'd had a scythe, he would have been mistaken for the grim reaper. Hope knew he was having a bad day.

"I think I might have made my presence known," said Max, the ghost.

2

Hope sat at the table while Cori headed for her room. "Time for voice practice," the teen told them.

"All right," Hope said to the ghost when her daughter had left the kitchen with the cat trotting behind her. "What did you do, Max?"

"You know I'm in the middle of a rather daunting editing job."

Max wanted to be useful so he often took contract jobs from online websites. By interacting online, no one knew he was a ghost.

Max said, "Seven books, all of which need extensive work. I can't begin to express my consternation, especially when my employer doesn't adhere to basic English rules. The person believes that rules don't count. I would agree, if the text, as written, conveyed any sort of meaning. One must read a paragraph multiple times, placing the commas and punctuation where needed, before the paragraph makes a modicum of sense. In most of my jobs, I do not change the words involved. That is the writer's prerogative. But these books are written at a grade school level. Multi-syllable words are banned."

"I understand," Hope said, "but how did you expose yourself?"

"Oh, right. I apologize, Mrs. Herring. I have been battling ignorance for far too long. To wit, I was prowling about the house working off the energy generated by the inane manuscript I was working on. I have found that walking around does soothe the soul. I was passing through the living room when I was startled by someone looking through the window."

Hope's eyes widened. "Who was it?"

"Who?"

"Yes. If it was the FedEx driver, it's no big deal. If it was the water meter reader, again nothing worry about. If it was a neighbor or friend, well, that's something else entirely."

"I see your point. Well, it was a neighbor. In fact, it was Adele Wells. Why she was looking in the window is beyond me. I suppose she wanted to make sure you were home, although I do not recall hearing the doorbell. That is not unusual, when I am lost in thought."

"So, what did you do?"

"I did what I had to do. I hurried from the room and into the kitchen. I also disappeared. A minute later, I spotted Adele peering through the kitchen window. She couldn't see me, but that hardly matters. She now knows some man is in your house. I suppose you'll have to invent some story to answer her curiosity, and I do apologize with all my might. I never intended to be seen."

"We are not going to worry about Adele. I'll tell her that you're a cousin, passing through Castle Park and stopping at my house, and you have since moved on."

"Will she believe that?" Max questioned.

"I think so. I mean, I didn't alert her to your visit because there was no need. My 'cousin' couldn't hang around."

"Or I could become your cousin and make myself visible to Adele and other people you view as harmless," the ghost suggested.

Hope shook her head. "The problem with living a lie is that you're living a lie. Liars are rarely smart enough to remember all the lies they tell. It's far better to keep your lies to the bare minimum."

"A wise strategy, Mrs. Herring. I shall adhere to it. My presence will remain unknown, except by you and Cori." Max stood. "And I need to get back to work. The errors in the manuscripts won't fix themselves."

"Take regular breaks," Hope said, "otherwise, you'll burn out. I suppose ghosts burn out too."

"We can. I'm sure of that. Good day to you, Mrs. Herring."

Max faded to nothing leaving Hope to ponder his metamorphosis from house ghost to reliable friend. When Max had been murdered in the house more than a hundred years ago, he had been about the same age as Hope was now ... in his mid-forties. The ghost didn't want to cross over until he'd solved the mystery of who had killed him. It took time, but Hope was able to figure it out with Max's help. The ghost was free to go now, but he still lingered, and she was grateful for that.

If Hope were honest, she would say that Max had become her best friend. She smiled at that. After all the years of being married, teaching, and raising a child, her best friend was a ghost.

Go figure.

At bedtime, Hope checked on Cori. The voice practice was over, but Cori now worked at the keyboard she had been given by the school music instructor, a gay man who was murdered by a jealous husband.

"Time for bed," Hope said.

"In a minute," Cori answered pushing her long brown hair over her shoulder. "I want to get this chord right."

"Enough is enough. Tomorrow will give you plenty of time for perfection."

"There's never enough time for perfection, Mom. Norrie told me that. We can get very close to it, maybe get a glimpse of it, but we can never get to it. Norrie believes that's good enough. I'm not so sure."

"I believe there's a school of thought that says achieving perfection finishes your life. After all, perfection can't be improved on so what's the sense in continued effort?"

"Take up another task? I mean, you can always look to be good at something else."

"Maybe. In any case, it's bedtime. By the way, have you gone online and looked at the books you'll need for classes this year?"

"Not yet. I don't want to get depressed about

school starting. Norrie says she thinks some people want to be depressed. It's a way to get attention."

"What do you think?"

"I think some kids like to show how depressed they are. I think they want the other kids to feel sorry for them."

"You're probably right. People who flaunt their sadness might be simply looking for some sort of validation, but there are lots and lots of people who actually suffer from depression. Depression should never be minimized. And that said, this discussion is over for the night. Sleep now. Tomorrow, we'll go shopping for school clothes."

"Really? Great. I've been looking online, but it's better if you can try them on before you buy."

"Exactly. Sleep well." She hugged her daughter.

In bed, Hope found it hard to sleep. She tossed and turned wondering if Cori was on the right track. She wished there were some sort of device that could gauge mood, like a thermometer for feelings. Place it on a person's forehead and know if they're happy or sad. Since there was no such device, Hope needed to come up with some other method. What could she do?

Allison Crush, Dr. Allison Crush.

The name conjured up the person, a thirty-something psychologist who was a contracted counselor for some troubled students at the middle school and high school. Allison was a regular on a morning TV show broadcast from Wilmington. Once or twice a week, she would give advice to the viewers about the dangers of not taking care of negative feelings and actions.

Credentialed with a Ph.D. and experienced, Allison might be the perfect sounding board for Cori. Hope might be too close, and Cori's voice coach and manager were focused on performance and ... money. Few people could prevent money from turning their vision green. Allison would be different. She was a professional. She would do no harm. Better, she would be at the school on a fairly regular basis.

Cost?

Hope would worry about that later. For the moment, she simply wanted her daughter to be happy.

A few days later, Hope was up to her elbows in flour. Saturday mornings found her at the Butter Up Bakery where she produced the needed cakes for the upcoming week. Hope had taken the job shortly after moving to Castle Park and while she was no longer so desperate for the money, she did enjoy the work. It was something totally different from teaching. More importantly, she had become friends with Edsel, the owner. That was enough to get Hope out of the house.

"Question," Edsel said.

Hope smiled at the stout, strong woman who baked like a dream and managed to keep all her customers happy.

"Answer," Hope replied. "I hope they match."

Edsel chuckled. "I just had a request for a Goth cake."

"Goth? As in the kids who go around dressed in black?"

"Yes, and with black fingernails and lipstick."

"Okay, I can do it. Devil's food cake, black icing, and blacker letters. Is this a birthday cake?"

"I don't think so. She mentioned that her daughter's therapist thought the cake would help her daughter realize that she doesn't have to be ashamed of her Goth stuff. Personally, I think it's a bunch of hooey, but there you go."

Hope laughed. "Tell your customer that I'll make the cake. Ask her what sort of greeting or lettering she wants."

"I'll get it in writing, and I'm going to charge her double." Edsel winked.

Hope would make the cake, and the child involved would like it. Perhaps, it would do some good.

Cori met her mother in the kitchen as soon as Hope walked through the door.

"We have to go to Norrie's," Cori said. "Right now."

"Wait. Tell me why we have to go now."

"She's not answering her phone, and she always answers her phone. Something has happened to her. We have to go and help her."

"Stop and think, Cori. If something did happen to her, it would be faster and wiser to send the police to Norrie's house. They can be there in minutes, and they would have the ability to help."

"You're not listening. We have to do it because we're her friends. The police will just mess up things."

"Let's suppose that we do go, and we do find that she's fallen or something. What would we do?"

"Take her to the hospital."

"No, we would call 911 because the EMTs know a lot more about transporting and caring for injured people. And they have an ambulance. They can treat Norrie on the way to the hospital."

Cori frowned. "She's my voice coach. The first one I had was murdered."

Hope stared at the teen. "You think Norrie might have been murdered?"

"People are always murdered around us, Mom. You're always solving one murder or two. Is it so far-fetched to think that something bad has happened to Norrie? I mean, we're practically black crows or something."

When they'd first moved to Castle Park, Hope met the local law enforcement officer Detective Derrick Robinson, and because of the help she'd given him on a case, they'd become friends and he often turned to her for assistance.

"I see your point. All right, you have five minutes to get ready."

As Cori turned, Hope grabbed her shoulder and turned her around.

"We're doing this for two reasons," Hope said. "We're going to check on your coach and friend because she hasn't answered her phone. That's unusual and deserves some attention. We are not going because we think she's been murdered. Do you understand? Put that thought out of your head. You are not cursed, and neither am I. We're going to prove that today. Now, go get ready. Five minutes."

Cori ran off leaving Hope to wonder if she was doing the right thing. The last thing she needed was for her level-headed daughter to transform into some kind of Chicken Little. The sky couldn't always be falling, no matter how many murders Hope had become involved with.

In the car, Hope watched as Cori tried calling Norrie repeatedly.

"That won't do any good," Hope said. "There's a good chance Norrie is out of the house and busy."

"I have to keep trying."

"No, you have to think. What's our mantra?"

"Fear keeps you from thinking."

"Exactly. So, if you're scared to death, you won't be able to think which is a human's greatest asset. Don't hamstring yourself by being frightened."

"I can't help it. I know something bad has happened. I can feel it."

"Think, Cori, think."

"That's not what Norrie says. She says I have to feel the music, the song. She says there are a lot of technically proficient singers. The great ones not only do all the right things, but they add feeling. The audience is entranced because they feel also. Bad singers can't get the audience to feel."

"There's a time and place for feeling, but when

you're scared, you have to use your head. I won't argue with your coach. I just want you to be able to control your feelings."

"I will."

Norrie's farmhouse looked the same as always. As soon as the SUV stopped, Cori was out the door and running. She vaulted onto the porch and rang the doorbell. Hope followed, as Cori tried the door.

"Locked." Cori pounded on the door with her small fist. "Norrie! Norrie!"

Hope moved to the side and looked through a window. While nothing seemed to be disturbed, she didn't spot Norrie either.

"Back door." Cori ran off the porch.

Hope followed watching the teen round the corner. In a way, Hope wished her daughter would react as fast when there was work to be done.

When Hope went around to the back of the house, she saw the backdoor was open and there was no sign of Cori. Hope walked into the kitchen and found her daughter staring. She walked to Cori's side and realized why the teen was shaking.

On the floor was a pool of red blood.

Hope's heart dropped.

3

Cori stared at the red, not-yet-congealed blood.

"Call 911," Hope told her.

Cori didn't move.

Hope held her daughter's shoulder and turned her away from the blood. "We aren't going to panic. Call 911. Do you understand?"

Cori nodded.

Hope nudged her toward the door. "Go outside. You'll get better reception."

"What? Where are you going?"

"I'm going to go through the house. If she's hurt, I'll help. You wait for the police."

Hope watched until Cori was safely out of the house, then she turned and hurried through the kitchen. If Norrie was hurt, Hope would have to find her quickly.

There were bloody towels in the downstairs half-bath. Hope found a few drops on the way to the front door. As she stepped onto the porch, she noticed a few more drops on the wooden deck. Hope was puzzled. If Norrie had come this far, where was she? Her vehicle was parked to one side of the driveway.

Where could she be?

Had she started walking? Was she disoriented? Did she just trudge off? If it was a head injury, she might not be thinking very well. A single thought might propel her in any direction. Hope peered all around. Which way did she go?

Cori charged around the corner, waving her phone.

"The police have already been here," Cori said. "They took her to the hospital."

"Which one?"

"The one in Burgaw."

"Want to make a visit?"

Cori smiled. "Yeah, I think I do."

Hope grinned. "Okay. Let's go say hey to Norrie."

Hope and Cori found Norrie in her own hospital room. The older woman's head was wrapped in gauze and tape, but her eyes were bright and her smile was warm.

"You found me," Norrie said weakly.

Cori ran to the bed and wrapped her arms around the woman.

"Careful," Norrie told her. "I hit my head."

"Oh, oh, yeah." Cori backed off a little.

Hope moved to the bed and took Norrie's hand. "What happened?"

"I fell," Norrie replied. "But I should probably start at the beginning. I was gardening, and I suppose I was not fully hydrated. The heat and humidity got to me. I became lightheaded. I went inside. That was when I became dizzy. I fell and hit my head. I'm not sure how long I was on the floor bleeding, but it was for some time. I managed to get to my feet and call for help. I met them at the door. That's how I got here."

"I'm glad you were aware enough to call for help," Hope said. "Cori was the one who insisted on going to your house to see if you were all right."

"I'm glad she did. You might have found me on the floor."

"How long will you be here?" Cori asked.

"Overnight at least for observation, although the

x-ray showed no concussion or swelling. I suppose it was just my thin skin that did the bleeding."

"Do you have a ride home?" Hope asked.

"Not yet."

"When you're ready, call us. We'll pick you up."

"I'll do that." Norrie turned to Cori. "You, my dear, must continue to practice. I may be unavailable for a few days, but that doesn't mean you're on vacation."

Cori grinned. "No? You're kidding, right. I have to keep going even when you're not around?"

"She's kidding with you," Hope told the woman.

"I'm aware of that." Norrie smiled. "Cori knows that practice is the key."

At that moment, a woman in a lab coat entered. Hope recognized the woman who smiled at them.

"Hello, I'm Allison Crush," the psychologist said before she turned to Norrie. "And you must be Norrie."

Allison Crush had dark brown eyes and was thin and attractive. Her long honey-colored hair was pulled back into a ponytail. Hope guessed that Allison used skin moisturizers and creams on a nightly basis. She might have had some cosmetic surgery as her eyes seemed bigger than normal.

Hope wasn't sure, which spoke volumes about how proficient the surgeon had been. Hope guessed Allison was at least forty, but it was hard to tell.

"Dr. Crush," Norrie said, "meet Cori, the girl I give voice lessons to, and Hope, Cori's mother. She's the detective."

Hope stepped forward to shake Allison's hand. The psychologist's grip was firm.

"Nice to meet you," Allison said. "I'm part of the hospital team that evaluates head trauma. I'll be asking Norrie some questions."

"She seems fine to me," Cori said.

"That's good to know. Do you mind if I have Norrie for a few minutes?"

"We're just leaving," Hope said.

"Thank you," Allison said. "See you at school."

Hope stared a moment. "You work with some of the students at the school, don't you?"

"Adolescents need help every bit as much as older people," Allison said. "Perhaps more so."

"I believe you're right. See you at school then."

Hope walked with Cori out of the hospital.

"Do you think I need a different coach?" Cori asked.

"Do you want a different coach?"

"No, but I was thinking that if Norrie can't teach me, I would have to find someone new."

"You're thinking ahead, but you're too far ahead. It was one dizzy moment. You can't change plans and horses after one event."

"You're right. I'll just have to keep an eye on her."

"An eye?"

"You know, if she starts to forget things or repeat lessons or falls asleep. Old people things."

"Old people, like me?"

"You're not old, Mom. I don't think you'll ever be old, not that way. Your brain is always working."

"Sometimes, that's not enough. People grow old and they slow down. That's a fact of life."

"By the time I'm old, they'll have computer chips you can add to your brain, so you don't ever slow down."

"That's sci-fi stuff, Cori. Your best bet for being fully aware as you age is to eat, drink, and sleep to your advantage. Nothing destroys a brain faster or more thoroughly than no exercise, not enough sleep, nothing to engage you, and using drugs, and that includes alcohol."

"Don't worry. I'm not going to become some physical and mental wreck."

"Just remember that it takes good habits to avoid the pitfalls of life."

Hope found Max in the attic office with Bijou on his lap. He was busy on his computer, but he turned as soon as she entered.

"I have found my second wind," Max said. "The editing is going far better than I had feared. How is Cori's coach?"

"In the hospital. She fell and hit her head. She appears well enough to me, but I'm no doctor. They're keeping her for at least a day."

"Prudence is a necessary quality for a hospital. I have read blurbs about the most dreadful outcomes for some patients. Suing a hospital or doctor has become a pastime, has it not? I mean, in my day, no one would have sued a hospital. We were glad just to have some sort of medical service."

"People expect cures," Hope said. "When they don't get one, they get upset. We believe there's a pill or a surgery for every little ailment."

"We have not learned much, have we?" Max asked.

"We haven't learned to accept what the world throws at us. People want to believe that they can have perfect lives with no hint of pain and suffering, and big pharmaceutical companies sometimes push that lie. Take your medicine, and you will smell roses and smile at blue skies."

Max nodded. "I have a theory that the fall of empires comes from promises that cannot be kept. Citizens expect more and more for less and less because the politicians involved always promise more. When more is not forthcoming, the society falls apart."

"That would be par for the course. If we don't ever experience hardship, how will we know when times are good?"

"I'm afraid I won't be around to witness the unraveling of this great country."

"Going somewhere, Max?"

"Not yet, but that is inevitable, Mrs. Herring. I have already succeeded. We have accomplished the task that kept me in this house."

Hope's heart sank. "You can't leave yet. Cori would never forgive you."

"No, no, not yet. I can choose when to move along. This is not the time. Yet."

"Good. I'll leave you to your manuscript."

Max saluted and turned to the computer. Hope was happy Max had found a job. It was a reason for him to stay with her and Cori. While she knew he couldn't exist as a ghost forever, she wasn't ready for him to leave. He had become a true companion and she would miss him terribly. Hope knew he was someone who could never be replaced.

The next day, Hope drove Cori to Norrie's farmhouse, and, together, they cleaned up the mess in the kitchen. They had cleared it with Norrie, who was staying one more day in the hospital. Her doctors wanted to run a few more tests. They wanted to be certain that her dizziness was caused by dehydration and not a blood pressure or some other issue.

"You think we'll able to get rid of the stain?" Cori asked, as she looked down at the kitchen floor.

"I'm not sure," Hope answered. "I don't know how porous the tiles are. If the blood seeped in, then getting it out might be hard."

"Can we replace the tiles?"

"Sure, if we can find the right pattern. With luck, there were a few extra around when the floor was laid. Of course, the tiles might have faded a bit under the sun. A new tile will look like a new tile. Replacement is better left to a professional."

"Sunlight fades everything, doesn't it?"

"The rays are more powerful than you think. That's why there's a lot of skin cancer these days. A lot of people spent a lot of time in the sun when they were young. The damage was done early."

"Yeah, but doesn't sunlight have vitamin E or something?"

"Vitamin D, and it's created in the body when there's sufficient sunshine. There are supplements, too. A lot of doctors recommend a daily dose of vitamin D."

"Doesn't it strike you as odd that sunlight can help by making D, and at the same time damage your skin so you might get cancer?"

"Moderation, I guess. All things in moderation. You get enough sun but not too much. You drink a little bit of alcohol but not too much. You eat enough but not so much that you become overweight. Of course, we humans aren't really good at moderation."

"You're right. Moderation is the best way. There are girls in my class who don't eat enough. They're really skinny, too skinny."

"We live on a pendulum. It swings one way, and we hang on until it decides to stop and swing the other way."

"Singing is like that." Cori smiled. "There are sweet spots where every note is near perfect, but it doesn't last."

"Well, almost perfect is pretty darned good." Hope stared down at the tiles. "I don't think we're going to get the stain out. Over time, it won't be so noticeable. Norrie will get used to it. Humans are very good at adjusting to changes in their environment. A month of two of new details, and the old environment is hard to remember."

Cori nodded. "Yeah, I know how that goes."

"Put all the dirty towels and rags in a plastic bag. We'll wash them at our house and bring them back."

"Roger that."

Hope made sure the house was secure before they drove off. While Norrie thought she would be getting out of the hospital the next day, there was no certainty of that. If the doctors discovered something... Hope didn't want to think about that. Norrie was going to be just fine. Fewer hours in the garden under the North Carolina sun would keep her out of the hospital.

At home, Hope started the washer. She stepped back just as Max appeared.

"Mrs. Herring, congratulate me. I finished the editing gig. The contractor was so pleased that he gave me a bonus. How about that? I wasn't aware he could do that."

"If he gives you a good rating, you may well find

more people who want to hire you. If that's the case, make sure you ask for enough money."

"I will, Mrs. Herring, I will."

Cori burst into the laundry room. "Mom, you have to help."

"Slow down, Cori. Help with what?"

"I have to join a church."

4

Hope frowned. "Join a church? Why?"

"I read online that a lot of singers got their start in church, in the choir. They were so good they became soloists. Word got around, and they were offered record deals."

"I see. And you think this could happen to you?"

"I saw it in my own life," Max said. "The churches were filled with good voices, although mine was never anything to garner praise."

"Exactly," Cori said. "It's a way to get wedding and party gigs."

"All right," Hope said. "I see your point. What church do you want to join?"

"I don't know. That's where I need help. I don't

want a church that demands too much, if you know what I mean."

"You can't join a congregation just to sing. That's the wrong reason, and it will lead to dissatisfaction for both you and the church. So, I recommend you do some research and discover just what joining entails. It's generally a lot more than what you might think."

Cori nodded. "You don't have any suggestions?"

"Religion is a personal thing. Decide on what your core beliefs are and find a church that fits. Of course, it will help if you find one that needs a good voice."

"I have no recommendations," Max said. "The church I attended has changed dramatically since I attended. I must confess that I am woefully out of touch."

"I'll figure it out," Cori said, "but, if either of you happen onto something, I'm open to suggestions."

Cori left, and Hope faced Max. "What do you think?"

"I'm not sure, Mrs. Herring. I have little experience with music careers or church singing. I realize that many successful singers started in the choir, but that is the extent of my knowledge. I do believe an introduction to the religious experience might prove helpful. Religion often teaches that we all answer to a higher power. Also, we learn that we have an obligation to do good and avoid evil."

"You make a good point. I've always emphasized good over bad, but Cori's approaching the age when she won't listen."

"I'm sure you and Cori will figure out what she needs. Beware of a Svengali."

"Someone who will seem infallible to her?"

"Exactly. The young are more easily persuaded than the old."

"I'll remember that."

"I'm off to hunt down my next gig," Max said. "Wish me luck."

"Good luck, Max."

With a nod, Max vanished, and Hope smiled. Max's arrivals and departures would never cease to amaze her.

The next day, Hope checked on Norrie, who had returned to her house. Norrie wanted to pay her for the cleanup, but Hope wouldn't accept a nickel. She and Cori had returned the house to normality because it was the right thing to do. That was reward enough. Norrie assured Hope that voice lessons would resume immediately, as her doctors had placed no restrictions on her. Business as usual was the order of the day. Hope did not raise the church question. That was something Cori would have to wrestle with on her own time.

The first day of the new school year started with an assembly. The students sat in the gym bleachers, while the principal introduced the support staff and cited the rules and regulations of the school. For some of the students, the speech was old hat. Others needed to know about the people and services provided. Allison Crush was introduced, and more than one student clapped. The principal informed the crowd that Allison would provide individual counseling upon request. Hope smiled at that. Perhaps Allison could provide some advice regarding Cori's search for a suitable church.

The rest of the day passed without incident, and on the way home, Hope asked Cori about her search.

"I'm still gathering data," Cori said. "I don't know how long it will take, but I don't want to make a mistake. I'm thinking I should talk to the pastors or priests or whoever is in charge."

"That can be a good idea, but you must be careful. Religious leaders can be very capable salesmen. Their job is to recruit parishioners, so they tend to make everything sound rosy."

"I think I know what you're talking about. When

I do online searches, I'm bombarded by ads about this church or that preacher. A lot of them don't have real churches. They have virtual churches, ones you attend online. Just send some money, and you can be 'saved.'"

"That's not surprising. I suppose the virtual church was a big thing during the pandemic. If you can't attend in person, you can attend through the Internet. Now that I think about it, that was probably a godsend for many people who relied on their connection to a church."

"They also didn't have to dress up to go to church."

Hope laughed. "That would be a plus. Sit in a virtual pew in your pajamas."

Cori giggled. "That would be so sick."

Hope knew Cori was praising the idea, despite the language. She didn't try to keep up with teenage slang, but she couldn't help learning a few things.

"I don't pay much attention to the online churches," Cori said. "I'm not sure they're all that reliable."

"Wait until artificial intelligence provides you with a virtual pastor. Not a real human, just an app that has been designed to provide answers to difficult questions."

Cori shook her head. "I don't think I would trust an app."

"Hey, I just had a thought. Do you think a school counselor can provide some input? I was thinking about Dr. Crush. She might know some facts about religion and good mental health that we don't know about."

"Cool. I can do that. I mean, I don't know everything, right?"

"No, you just think you do," Hope kidded.

"Right."

After the school day, Hope found Max in the throes of a new project. He was wearing a turban and long, white coat buttoned up the front. To Hope, he looked straight out of Delhi.

"Tell me." Hope gestured to the outfit.

"The client lives in Mumbai," Max said, "which used to be Bombay. The manuscript he sent is in Hindi, which the computer translates into English. I edit the English and translate back into Hindi. I work paragraph by paragraph, which I send back to the client. If it works, then it goes into the final product. If not, I have to massage the English until it translates into passable Hindi. Apparently, computer translating programs lack the 'nuances' of a human translator. Since I do not speak Hindi, I cannot be a reliable judge. This is a labor intensive project that isn't abetted by the huge time difference."

"I hope the compensation is good enough for your trouble."

"It is ... for now. Mrs. Herring, do you think I need a manager?"

"Manager? What makes you ask that?"

"Well, Cori has one, and she has a coach also. Her manager is like a gatekeeper, correct? Cori learns only of the offers that she qualifies for."

"That's correct, Max. Her manager also tries to find gigs for Cori. Are you so popular that you need a manager?"

"Honestly, I have to admit that I am not smothered by offers."

"You have to remember that you have to pay a manager. Would a gatekeeper be worth ten percent of your earnings?"

"I see your point. I don't make enough the way it is. The host site takes its cut first. I suppose I shall have to simply put up with the inconveniences."

"Luckily, you can accommodate any time zone."

"That is a plus, isn't it?"

The next day, Hope checked with Norrie. Cori's lesson was good to go, if Hope could pick up Norrie at the medical building where her doctor had an office. Norrie wasn't yet cleared to drive. A ride share company had provided a way to the office.

Because of the air conditioning, Hope and Cori waited in the building. They were alone, except for a pudgy, bald man in spectacles, who never looked up from his phone. Casually dressed, he made Hope wonder what ailed him.

Norrie was with someone when she emerged from the examination rooms. With her was a tall, thin woman with black-rimmed glasses. Her black hair was pulled back in a bun, and she wore slacks and a top. The stethoscope around her neck probably meant she was a doctor.

The bald man jumped out of his seat as soon as he spotted the doctor.

"Gerald," the doctor asked, "what are you doing here?"

"Pamela, we need to talk."

"Can't it wait? I have a patient here."

Gerald shook his head. "This is serious."

Pamela nodded. "Go ahead and wait in my office."

Gerald nodded and disappeared through a door. Pamela's frown became a smile as she turned to Hope and Cori.

"Let me introduce Dr. Callier," Norrie said. "She just told me I could drive."

Pamela shook hands with Cori and then Hope. "Norrie can drive if she feels up to it," the doctor said. "Just some short trips during the day for a few weeks."

"I never drive at night anyway," Norrie said.

"I don't either, if I can help it," Hope said.

Pamela focused on Cori. "So, you're the prodigy Norrie brags about."

"I'm not that good," Cori said. "I just sing easy songs."

"Don't listen to her," Norrie said. "Cori has a wonderful voice, and she's getting better all the time. I have great hopes for her."

"I believe Norrie," Pamela said. "She knows what she's talking about. It was nice meeting you both. I have to get back to work." She turned to Norrie. "You know what to do and what to avoid. Call, if you have any problems."

"Of course, Dr. Callier. Don't be upset, if you don't see me or hear from me for a while," Norrie grinned.

"I won't mind." With a smile, Pamela walked away.

"Please, get me home," Norrie told Hope. "I can't

help but think that a doctor's office is for sick people."

"I don't think the doctor's patients are contagious," Hope said, "but, I share your attitude. Time to go."

"Have you been practicing?" Norrie asked Cori, as they left.

"I have," Cori answered. "Even if I do drive my mother crazy."

Norrie chuckled. "A good kind of crazy."

Hope waited on the patio during Cori's lesson. The lemonade was cold and refreshing, and a breeze kept the heat at bay. She checked her email and texts to see if any of her students were having difficulty with the assigned homework. There was a note from a girl who included a solution to a problem. Isabella came from a family with six children, and she asked for help almost daily. Hope knew that Isabella didn't need the help. She simply wanted attention and a bit of praise that was usually heaped on her athletic brothers. Hope understood, and she was glad to help. As usual, Isabella had the correct answer. She deserved a bit of support. Hope sent a short note, complete with a smiling emoji.

Was Cori like Isabella?

Hope couldn't help but wonder if Cori's pursuit

of a singing career wasn't simply a plea for attention. No, Hope couldn't really believe that. Her daughter had the talent. As an only child, she didn't suffer from lack of attention. She had a mother and a ghost to interact with. So, the danger Hope could see was that Cori wouldn't make it.

But was that a bad thing?

Hope knew that people needed to fail. They needed to understand that failure was not the end of the world. They needed to be able to change direction if their current path ended. Resilience was, perhaps, the most important lesson a person could learn. In Hope's opinion, the people who enjoyed life the most were the ones who could pick up a new job or hobby in a few minutes. They didn't wallow in self-pity or retreat into a shell.

Failure. It could be a good thing—or so she thought.

Hope and Cori hadn't even been home for an hour before Norrie called.

"Norrie," Hope said. "Did we forget something?"

"No, no, my doctor called."

Hope bit her lip in anticipation of bad news.

"She wants to talk to you," Norrie said.

Hope's eyes widened.

5

"Dr. Callie is out on the patio," Norrie said.

"Any idea what she wants to talk to me about?" Hope asked.

Norrie shook her head. "It's something personal. There's iced tea on the table."

Hope turned to Cori. "I'll be outside with the doctor."

"Take your time," Norrie said. "Cori and I will be fine."

Dark clouds bubbled up in the distance telling Hope that the storms would be arriving before long. One of the things she missed about Ohio, where she had lived before, was the weather pattern. If she wanted to know what was coming, she simply looked west. Weather ran west to east ... it was simple. North Carolina was not so accommodating. A lot of storms moved up the coast and those storms could produce rain, lots of rain.

Pam Callier faced the clouds. She wore a blouse and slacks, as if she had come straight from her office. She spoke as soon as Hope sat.

"First," Pam said, "I'm not exactly sure why I want to talk to you. I mean, this has nothing to do with school, or baking cakes, or even Norrie's head trauma. It's about the other stuff you do."

Hope was surprised that Pam knew as much as she did. "Other stuff?"

"Everyone around here calls you the Sherlock of the South. Most people think you could solve the mystery of the Sphinx, if you put your mind to it."

Hope shook her head. "My talents are woefully exaggerated. I have had the opportunity to unravel a few murders, mostly because I had to. I was considered a possible suspect. Facing a stint in prison is a prime motivator."

"I understand motivation. I became a doctor because my father suffered from Parkinson's disease. I was in high school when his hands began to shake. By the time I finished med school, he was having problems walking and talking. I became a brain specialist because I wanted to save him. I couldn't.

His symptoms were too far advanced. It wasn't that I didn't try. I simply ran of time."

"We all do. Time doesn't wait for us. Before you know it, you're looking in the mirror and wondering who that old, wrinkled person is."

Pam chuckled. "Don't remind me. By the way, Norrie tells me that your daughter is quite a singer. Congratulations. I can't carry a tune in a bucket, but then I don't have the ear for music either. I pretty much limit my listening to podcasts."

"Cori can sing, but the world is full of girls who can sing. Does she have what it takes to be really, really good? The verdict is out on that. I'm pretty sure I don't have that kind of single-purpose mind. I want Cori to take pride in developing a skill and enjoy what she does, no matter the outcome."

"A very good way to look at life. But, enough of that. What do you know about physician partnerships?"

"Not much. I'm assuming they're the wave of the future. The day of the independent family doctor appears to be over."

"Yeah, it works a lot like a law firm. Generally, one of the doctors also runs the partnership, but sometimes the doctors will hire a manager. Then, there are the hybrids like the one I'm in. We have a leading partner, but we also have an accountant who helps with the books. You know, don't put all your eggs in one basket. There are some rules about who can spend what. Expenditures require more than one signature."

"I understand the architecture, although I'm glad I don't have to partner with a bunch of teachers. In my experience, every teacher thinks he or she knows more than anyone else." Hope chuckled.

"Doctors are no different. They're trained to offer opinions, and boy, do they. It's a wonder they're all not billionaires. You would think they invented electric vehicles and solar panels."

Hope said, "I believe there's a term for people who believe they're way above average. Some psychologists did a study. While it's statistically impossible for everyone to be above average, almost everyone thinks they are."

"I'm no different, I guess. I like to think I'm smarter than average."

"I'm sure you are." Hope poured herself more iced tea. "What is it you want to talk about with me?"

"I told you; we have an accountant who keeps things in order. Gerald is very good at his work. He's a CPA, detail oriented. He came to me last week, and he was worried. He said there were funds missing. He didn't say how much, but it was substantial."

Hope raised an eyebrow. "That's never a good thing."

"No. Worse, he said that my signature was on some fraudulent checks."

"Fraudulent?"

"Yes, and I have to tell you that I did not sign those checks."

"If it's not your signature, that should be easy to prove."

"In our system, we have an electronic signature. I get sent a check, and if I agree with the amount and the payee, the check is signed electronically. In many cases, the check is not mailed. The money is wire transferred to the payee."

"So, someone pretended to be you?"

Pam nodded. "But, not for all the checks or payments. Only for a select few. They were mixed in with the regular items, so neither Gerald nor I flagged them. And, once a check is signed, it disappears off my screen. I have no need to see it again."

"How did Gerald know it wasn't you?"

"He didn't. As far as he could see, I had signed the checks. It was only when I pointed out that some of the checks were signed while I was on vacation that he started to wonder."

Hope said, "In today's world, being on vacation doesn't mean you're out of touch. The web is everywhere."

"He knows that. And I know I can't really prove I wasn't the one at the keyboard, but it wasn't me. You have to believe that."

Hope studied the doctor wondering if Pam was telling the truth. Certainly, it would be easy to claim innocence especially when the crimes were perpetrated by computer.

"I do believe it," Hope said, "for now. I don't think you'd ask for my advice if you were guilty. You'd hire a clever attorney."

"Oh, I've already scouted the local firms. So far, I haven't found anyone I want to trust."

"The first question is how did someone find your password?" Hope asked the doctor.

"It was on a sticky note under my keyboard." The doctor looked pained. "I know, neither original nor secure."

"In your office?"

Pam nodded. "I thought that would provide some protection."

"Who had access to your office?"

"Who didn't? Doctors, nurses, assistants, even some patients, and, of course, the cleaning staff."

"Of those who had access, how many would be able to manipulate the payment system?"

"Not that many, but anyone with a fair knowledge of systems would be able to do some damage."

Hope nodded. "So, the suspect pool is large and there's not a good way to whittle out a large number of them."

"Fair enough. If you go to limiting possible suspects, you're liable to go right past the criminal."

Hope asked another question, "On the other end, has Gerald been able to track down the recipients of the money?"

Pam bit her lip, as color filled her cheeks. "So far, he has found two that have my name as the owner. I swear I know absolutely nothing about these sham corporations. Gerald said they were probably created online by one of those virtual law offices. I was surprised at how easy it is to register a corporation in our state."

"Everything done without anyone shaking hands with another human?"

"Exactly. Lies on top of lies on top of lies."

For a few seconds, Hope thought about the issue. "I'm supposing that once the money reached one of those fake businesses, it was quickly siphoned off to some offshore accounts?"

"Gerald hasn't tracked it that far yet. There is some indication that the money was paid out in cash. Small amounts, less than ten thousand. Trying to find someone who might remember the transactions is proving difficult."

"Have you talked extensively to Gerald?"

"No, he doesn't trust me. I can't say I blame him. If we traded places, I wouldn't trust me either."

"That doesn't speak well of you," Hope observed.

"I know when I'm in trouble. I'm not some idiot who believes in the tooth fairy. I don't want to go to prison for something I didn't do. Any suggestions?"

"When is Gerald going to the authorities?"

"Next week, I think. He's gone about as far as he can on his own. He's talking about a private investigation firm also."

"Before he does that, you need to get him on your side. It will help immensely if he says he doesn't believe you took the money."

"I've tried, but Gerald is no idiot either. He knows that if he says it's someone else, then people will think he and I were stealing together."

"Is there any evidence of that?"

"I think he found evidence that one corporation was in his name," Pamela said.

"Someone really wanted to muddy the water, didn't they?"

Pam shook her head slowly. "Circular firing squad. If everyone is guilty, then no one is."

"All right, we'll get to personal enemies. Who hates you enough to frame you for this theft?"

"You know, I can't think of anyone who has access to my computer and hates me enough to frame me for the crime. Don't get me wrong. There are some former patients who were not happy with my work. A couple even sued. One wanted money, which she didn't get. The other thought I really did botch a job. I didn't, and the court agreed. Malpractice suits are a common occurrence in my profession. I'm a lucky doctor who hasn't been in court too many times."

"If I were you, I'd do a thorough analysis of everyone who could have used your password. A person you think has no reason to ruin you might have a very good, hidden reason. While the obvious are always vetted first, even friends and relatives have to be scrutinized sooner or later."

"I know, I know," Pamela said. "The people who

have your back also have a perfect avenue of attack. I hate to think someone close has done this."

"We all do. I won't kid you. Crimes like these are very difficult to solve without help from national organizations. The FBI and Treasury have access to all the transfer and check clearing facilities. It sometimes takes years, but they're often successful in tracking the money, even when it goes overseas."

With a sigh, Pamela leaned on the table. "I was hoping you'd have some kind of special insight that might save me a lot of time and effort."

"Sorry, there aren't any shortcuts. If you can't pinpoint the thief, then you have to dig."

Pam half smiled and shrugged. "The longest journey begins with a single step, doesn't it? By the way, Norrie is very attached to your daughter and to you. What you did for her can't be repaid. She's a good person, and she recognizes the good in others. Your daughter could have done much worse choosing a voice coach."

Hope smiled. "I'm aware of that. I know you're not allowed to share patient information, but is Norrie in good health?"

"For her age, she's in great health. I do believe it was a case of too much heat and not enough water. The heat and humidity here take their toll."

"You're right about that. Anything I should look for?"

"Just the usual. Forgetfulness, inattention, lack of involvement. The brain is a mystery for most of us. People with dementia often become adept at hiding it. They lie, of course, but more often, they nod and agree, and you think they understand, but they don't. They've learned what it takes to appear more engaged than they really are."

"I'll remember that ... maybe."

They both laughed, which made Hope feel a little better. She hadn't been able to offer much help, but sometimes, the best aid was a sympathetic ear.

Hope and Cori were halfway home before the teen spoke.

"Do I need to start looking for another coach?" Cori asked.

"Why would you ask that?"

"Well, you talked to Norrie's doctor for a long time. I thought maybe the doctor was giving you some bad news."

"It was bad news, but it has nothing to do with Norrie's condition. Before you ask, it's about a crime that's been committed, a non-murder so don't get anxious."

"Did you help?"

"Not really. The doctor had already done most of the things I suggested. All I can tell you is that it was a computer-generated crime, and there's no flesh and blood human to quiz."

"Bummer."

"Yeah, bummer."

Two days later, Hope was preparing pork chops for dinner when she got the call from her friend Detective Derrick Robinson.

Gerald Pantini was dead.

6

Detective Robinson drove slowly down the winding roads. Full dark had not yet arrived and the western sky was pink and beautiful. Hope knew why she was in the car, but she wanted to know more. The detective had to feed her some facts.

"What do we know?" Hope asked.

"Are you sure you want to be briefed before we get there?"

"I think I need some information about what you're thinking."

"All right," Derrick said. "As of right now, I'm leaning toward suicide. He overdosed, and he left a note."

"Then, I'd think you already have the solution."

"I do and I don't. For one thing, the note isn't

signed, although it appears to be in his handwriting. His wife verified that. She also said that the man was not suicidal. He had no reason to kill himself. Well, he was estranged from his wife, but that wasn't enough—in the wife's opinion. I'm guessing there are some skeletons in the closet that might provide motive, but we haven't found them yet."

Hope wondered if it was time to reveal what she knew about Pam and the missing funds. If Gerald's death was a suicide, then there might not be a reason to tell the detective ... yet. When Gerald's business was analyzed, the money angle would arise naturally. However, with the missing money in the open, would someone vote for homicide?

"I happen to know that Gerald had found a discrepancy in the books for a medical partnership business. He was trying to track down the missing funds. As far as I know he wasn't the thief."

Derrick raised an eyebrow and took a quick look at Hope. "You know this how?"

"A woman, a doctor, came to me because she was afraid she would be accused of embezzlement. Her electronic signature was on some of the fake payments."

"So, she might be glad Gerald is dead?"

"Not if she's innocent. She needed Gerald alive until he found the real thief."

"All right, tell me everything."

Hope spent the next five minutes explaining the connections between Gerald, Pamela, and Norrie. Detective Robinson listened, with only an occasional question, and at the end, he sighed.

"And I thought this was going to be a simple suicide."

"Sorry. I didn't want to burst your balloon, but you had to know. It changes how you look at things."

"Indeed, it does." He pulled the car to curbside. "We're here."

Gerald's house was in a failed golf community. Someone had bought the land across the road from the original nine-hole course and built a second nine and lined the fairways with lots. The idea was to sell the lots and pay for the golf upgrade. Gerald's house had been one of the first built. It was a two-story, red brick home with a long porch and pillars at the front. The house looked as if it had been around before the war between the states. The lots on either side were weed-covered and empty. Down the street a few more houses had been built, but the empty lots far outnumbered those with houses.

"What happened here?" Hope asked.

"Familiar story. This side of town was growing, when some people involved with the golf course decided to build a second nine and start a housing development. Then, they built the Interstate on the other side of town. Another group of people bought land over there and built their own golf-course community. The Interstate was the difference. The area isn't populated enough to support two courses so this one died. When we get inside, look out the back windows. You'll see the fairway has gone to seed. It's nothing but weeds and saplings."

"What a waste." Hope shook her head.

"Part of our economics," Derrick said. "We have winners and losers. What's important is that people want to move here. Every house that gets built, every child that goes to school, that's a good thing. Would most of us like to have two golf communities? Of course, but there's only so much money to go around."

The inside of the house was only half furnished. Hope guessed that it had been fully furnished at one point, but when the wife moved out, she took some furniture with her, leaving gaps in the carpet and discolored rectangles on the wall where paintings had been hung. That was the problem with breakups. The house became a metaphor for the marriage. It had come apart. Putting it back together would take time and patience.

"Looks weird, doesn't it?" the detective asked. "The only room that looks whole is Gerald's in-house office."

"That's where the body is?"

"Was. It's been moved to the morgue, but you'll be able to see enough in the office. If you need photos, we have them."

Gerald's office was at the rear of the house. His desk faced French doors and large windows that revealed what had once been a golf hole. Nature had redeemed the ground filling it with yellow dandelions, small pine saplings, and some tall, very ugly weeds. There was a sand trap that had its own fill of weeds and grass. Hope knew that at one time, the scene must have been very pretty.

"We found him at the desk," the detective said, "face down, a bottle of pills spilled across the blotter. The computer was running, but it was locked up. We're trying to find the password. His wife thinks she has it written down somewhere, but she can't find it."

Hope pointed to four oak filing cabinets against one wall. "What about those?"

"Locked. We had no need to unlock them, if it was a suicide."

"I see, and no need to assemble a suspect list."

"Exactly. Now, I suppose we'll have to open the file cabinets and see what we can see. Same with the computer. You know, this was a lot easier before you told me about the missing money."

"Sorry about that." Hope walked slowly around the room.

"Don't be. Chances are you're not the only person aware of the theft, so sooner or later, we were going to have to begin a more intense investigation."

"Did Gerald have another office besides this one?"

"Yes, he had one downtown. We haven't processed that one yet."

"Because it was thought to be a suicide?"

"Yeah." Derrick shook his head.

"You said the bottle was open and pills spilled over the blotter?"

"Yep, along with the unsigned note."

"Are there cameras? Security?"

"Nothing here," Derrick told her. "I think there are some cameras in his other office though."

Hope pointed to some wires sticking out of the

corner by the ceiling. "Think that might have been a camera?"

"Looks like it. So maybe there's a recording device around here somewhere?"

"The computer would do."

"Yeah, we have to open that up also. You know you're not making this any easier," Derrick kidded.

With a shrug, Hope said, "I just want to get to the truth."

"Which includes going through his files to determine who might have wanted him dead."

"Tox screen?"

Derrick was writing something in his notepad. "I'll hurry it along."

"Was Gerald ever arrested for illegal drugs or alcohol?"

"Not that I'm aware of, but again, our investigation was centered on Gerald taking his own life."

"How long has his wife been gone?" Hope asked.

"My understanding is approximately three months."

"Do you know why she left?"

"Not yet. I didn't ask the wife. I assume it was like so many others. These two got tired of each other."

"That's the usual reason." Hope looked at the top

of Gerald's desk. "Any complaints from his other clients? Anything in the past?"

"I'm not aware of anything. Would you be willing to go with me to his downtown office when I get a key?"

"I can do that." Hope nodded. "Who found the body?"

"His wife. She'd tried to reach him and couldn't. That was unusual, so she came out here and let herself in. She was pretty shaken up. She never thought Gerald was capable of killing himself."

"Suicides generally surprise a lot of people. You didn't happen to process this location, did you?"

He shook his head. "No, there was no need. I'll have the forensic team do a workup, but you know there's been some contamination since the body was discovered."

"Can't be helped. What about family? Did Gerald have family in the area besides his wife?"

"I believe he has a brother in Raleigh. Gerald moved here from Ohio. His wife was from here. She didn't like Ohio winters. I got that much from her."

"I don't blame her for that. I'm from Ohio, too. Of course, you do realize that it might well have been a suicide and we're doing all this work for nothing."

"That's part of my job. We always seem to drill

dry holes until we find the right person. To tell the truth, I would just as soon prove this was a suicide as not. I don't like the idea of some killer on the loose in Castle Park."

"I think we've seen all we can see for the moment. When you unlock the computer and the file cabinets, there'll be more to examine."

"I have to talk to that doctor, too," Derrick said. "She would have a motive to get rid of Gerald, although she would know that sooner or later some other accountant would discover the same crime."

"True, but at that point, she can blame Gerald for the crime. He committed suicide because he stole the money and was trying to lay the blame on her."

"Every criminal needs a fall guy. Come on, I'll drive you home."

Pulling out of the development, Hope asked a question. "Was Gerald in financial trouble? I mean, he's got a big house in a neighborhood that isn't going anywhere."

"His wife didn't think so, but she's been gone for about three months. If it's any consolation, he was making payments to her per their agreement."

"That's encouraging. I suppose we'll just have to wait and see."

"That's always the hardest part."

At home, Cori was sitting in the kitchen with Bijou on her lap. The teen glommed onto Hope as soon as she walked through the door.

"My manager called," Cori said. "She has a gig for me, but, she needs to talk to you first."

"Why is that?"

"I think she said it was in Florida."

Hope put her purse on the table. "You *think*? Did she say it was in Florida or not?"

"Well, it is in Florida, at Disneyworld. There's a kid band that needs a vocalist. It's an audition for a new show Disney is producing."

Hope looked up surprised. "A new show?"

"For the Disney channel. Seven episodes for the first season. If people like it, there will be a second season."

"I see. Which means you would have to be in Orlando in order to shoot the show."

Cori nodded. "My agent sent in my highlight reel to Disney. They think I might be just what they need."

"How many months will the shooting take?"

"I don't know, but a few. I mean I think we would be shooting every day for a while. Seven episodes is a lot."

"Exactly. I'm guessing you'd have a tutor for your

education, as well as someone to watch over you when I'm not there."

"You wouldn't be there?" Cori looked shocked.

"I have a job, Cori. Sure, you'll probably make more money than me, but my job is more secure. I can't take a few months off to go to Florida."

"I'd get to come home some weekends."

"I understand." Hope studied her daughter. "Do you really want this gig?"

"Yeah. It's a once-in-a-lifetime gig, Mom."

"No, it's not. Yes, it's a huge opportunity, but that doesn't mean there won't be more of them in the future."

Cori shook her head. "Not with Disney."

"Maybe not. I'll call Norrie," Hope said. "I'll see what can be worked out. I'm telling you now, though, if I don't feel good about this gig, you won't be able to do it. I'm not a stage mom who throws her daughter into the machine and waits for the money to come out."

"I know, Mom, and I was almost certain they weren't even going to call back."

Hope smiled. "Hey, who knows, if this works out, you might be set for life. We'll both be set for life. Sounds pretty good, doesn't it?"

Cori nodded; her face serious. "I remember once

when Dad was alive. He was working on some article or something. I asked him why he worked so hard. He said that whoever was paying him expected some real effort. He had to make it so good that the boss would never dream of searching for someone else to replace him. If Dad expected a big check, he had to put in big time work. Shoddy work might get him by once but only once. For Disney, I would have to put in the time."

"You would. Hard work would be the order of the day so finish your homework and your voice lessons. I'll call Norrie tomorrow."

Cori hugged her mother, and Hope held onto her daughter for an extra moment. She knew that Cori was moving on, blazing her own path through life.

Hope's phone chirped, and she answered.

"Hello, Pamela," Hope said.

7

Hope couldn't help but notice that Pamela's hands shook as she picked up the wine glass. Was the woman worried, nervous, or guilty?

"You know why I asked to see you." Pamela's eyes had dark circles under them. "Gerald is dead."

Hope nodded and looked out the window at the growing darkness, the shadows slipping out from under the trees. "Have you ever wondered about how the universe works? Every day, night comes. The sun disappears and darkness fills in behind it. Sure, science can explain it, but how did it all start? How did the planets align? How did people appear on this planet, a planet where they could survive? It seems too good to be chance. It's almost as if someone planned it all."

Pamela stared. "Are you saying someone planned Gerald's death?"

"It's possible that 'someone' might have been Gerald himself." Hope set down her wine glass.

Pamela's eyes went wide. "You mean suicide?"

"Do you find that jolting?" Hope questioned.

"I never took Gerald for the suicide type, but I suppose anyone could be pushed to it, if the stars aligned just right."

"There was a substantial amount of money missing," Hope reminded the woman.

"Yes, but he'd already pushed the criminal part of that away from himself. He wanted me to take the hit."

"You said you didn't do it."

"I didn't. I know you don't entirely believe me. I wouldn't, if I were you, but you probably don't think Gerald took the money either."

"Was he clever enough to use your signature to steal the funds?" Hope questioned.

"Clever enough? Sure, he knew the system as well as anyone. I'll tell you a little story about Gerald. He was an independent contractor so, on occasion, he would invite a client to dinner at a very nice restaurant. He liked steak. He would go over whatever business he had, pump the client for a referral, and pay for the meal. One time, we went to dinner and since we talked business, it was a deduction. Easy enough. That evening, he had one scotch too many. He liked scotch, as long as it was deductible. The next day, he called me. He had lost the receipt. Did *I* have it? No, I hadn't paid so I didn't have the receipt. He was anxious because the meal was expensive, given the drinks we had. I told him what I thought the meal cost and he agreed, but he still needed the receipt. I asked him if he really believed that the IRS would come after him for a few hundred dollars. Without a receipt, he wasn't going to book the expense. Now, would a man like that have the courage to steal thousands from his clients?"

Hope shook her head. "I believe you. Gerald might be able to fool us, but he wasn't that gifted an actor, was he?"

Pamela shook her head.

"Do you know what medications he was taking?"

"I don't know exactly, but I would guess he was on a statin and probably a blood pressure medication. Other than that, I have no idea."

"If someone sneaked some poison pills into his bottle, would he know the difference?"

"A man like Gerald might. He would probably

use one of those little plastic cases, where you load daily meds into their own little bin."

"Keeps people from missing a day or over-medicating."

Pamela said, "Oh, I'm all for whatever device is needed. I simply don't see Gerald as someone who would mistake a blue pill for a pink one."

Hope sipped her wine. "Let's suppose someone did poison him. Who would want him dead?"

"Me, but you already know that. I didn't kill him, but I suppose everyone will say that I did."

"Who else?"

"His wife, of course. You did know they were separated, right?"

Hope nodded.

"I'm guessing Gerald left sizable assets. He was good at pinching pennies. He always did the best by the partnership. I don't believe his wife came from money so she would have a gain."

"Go on. Brothers, sisters, clients?"

"I know nothing about his family. He wasn't from here. I suppose his family was like most. They all did their own thing until something went wrong. I don't recall him telling me about siblings, but that doesn't mean he didn't have any. As far as clients go, I remember one man who had a falling out with

Gerald. It had something to do with a missed filing of some sort. The man said it cost him a lot of money because his credit rating went to heck. That's all I know. Gerald wasn't one to share stories."

"It probably doesn't matter. There's no evidence of murder at this point."

Pamela poured more wine into her glass.

"How about the other partners in your medical practice?" Hope asked. "Did anyone have a problem with Gerald?"

"There were some questions from time to time, but no one had a reason to want him dead, not as far as I could see. Of course, you would have to ask them separately."

"No need at the moment. I'm just fishing. Was Gerald devoted to his wife?"

"As far as I knew. They would come to the annual Christmas party for the partners. They got along, at least in public. Did she look like the murdering type? Not to my eye, but then, who does?"

"Murderers who look like murderers don't last long."

Pamela sighed. "I'll drink to that."

After a few more minutes, Hope changed the subject to something other than Gerald and when Pamela finished her wine, she left. Hope didn't feel she'd learned anything from the doctor who simply wanted to broadcast her innocence.

"Do you think I should try my hand at writing?" Max asked when Hope entered the attic office to find the ghost and the cat sitting together in an upholstered chair.

"Do you want to write?"

"I feel I have the skills to write. I mean, I don't think I'm going to write another Huckleberry Finn or Lord Jim, but I might be able to fashion a reasonable mystery."

"I'm sure you could. After all, you're now an accomplished editor."

"My editing does not exactly set the world on fire. However, the books I'm asked to improve are poorly designed and hardly worth reading. I mean, when the cats and dogs talk to the main character, you can't have a serious mystery, can you?"

"I don't agree. Those sorts of stories are meant for people who don't want a lot of graphic violence. A good mystery can be crafted with cats and dogs in them. I can't say I blame the readers. Modern fiction and movies seem to exist for the lurid."

"Yes, indeed. I was thinking something along the lines of what Agatha Christie might write. You know, polite stories where people die, but they don't die horrible deaths. Well, nothing described as horrible. A bullet of course, and poison to be sure, but no one gets tortured for ten pages."

"As I recall the dialogue doesn't contain slang or curses. That alone might be enough to sell your book."

Max grinned. "You've talked me into it. Might I ask you to help, should I become stalled at some point? You do have a mind for such things."

Hope smiled at the ghost. "I will be happy to help."

"Splendid. I shall begin with the murder and work back to the suspects. Seems like a good process."

"You'll do well, I'm sure."

Hope stopped by Cori's room where the teen was practicing on her keyboard. She had the sound turned down, so she wouldn't bother anyone.

"Time for bed," Hope said.

"Listen to this."

Cori turned up the volume and played a recognizable tune. Hope was amazed.

"When did you learn to do that?"

"Norrie's been teaching me. She says two talents are better than one."

"Lounge singer?"

Cori made a face. "Yuck. I hope not. I think it's easier to write songs if I can play piano."

"I'm sure that's true. It's late. You should head to bed."

"You're going to call tomorrow about the Disney gig?" Cori got up from the keyboard.

"Yes, I'll contact your manager."

"Thank you, Mom. I'd really like to try for this."

"Don't thank me yet. I might let you do it."

Cori laughed. "Wouldn't that be cool? Lottie might die of envy."

"Don't worry about Lottie. Is your homework finished?"

"All of it, even the research I have to do for my next paper."

"Where did all this diligence come from?"

"I've decided that I need to plan better so I can execute better. Like you said, it's work that we have to perform."

"I was thinking about athletes," Hope said. "Have you ever wondered how many times they execute a shot or jump or whatever in practice, so they can do it in a game?"

"It doesn't just happen, does it?"

"No. If you think about it, their best days on the

court or field probably don't coincide with a game. They're probably at their absolute best in practice."

Cori said, "I never thought about that."

"I guess that's because we rarely see them at practice. We watch the games. They're very good during the game, but they might be even better in practice." Hope leaned down to kiss her daughter. "Now I'll say goodnight."

With a wave, Hope went to her own room. In bed, she pushed aside Gerald and his death. More than likely, his demise would be ruled a suicide. The motivation for that would come out eventually. Everyone would go to the funeral and then move on. She needed to concentrate on Cori, on an offer that could well change the arc of her life. Working for Disney didn't guarantee success, but it was certainly a step up from singing the national anthem before a baseball game.

True to her word, Hope phoned the manager the next day. While the manager assured Hope that Cori would be well-supervised on the set, Hope knew the assurances were part of the pitch. Cori would have a tutor, so she wouldn't fall behind in her classes. She would have a governess who would stay with Cori all day and all night. Hope could talk to Cori every day, if that would help ease the anxiety. In short, every possible accommodation would be made—if Cori made the cut.

The cut.

"I won't sugarcoat this," the manager said. "Cori will be asked to do more than sing. She'll be asked to act and to dance. I am fully aware that she does not yet have those skills. That doesn't mean she won't get the role. It does mean that she will need to take lessons. No one learns to dance by watching Fred Astaire."

After the conversation, Hope was more wary then before. She hadn't anticipated dancing and acting lessons. She hadn't budgeted for those expenses either. She wondered how she was going to find the money—and the instructors. Certainly, there were charlatans around, people who would take the money and teach very little. The world was filled with scammers.

She could talk to Norrie. Norrie would probably know some reputable instructors, but were they within driving distance? Castle Park wasn't large. It didn't support a theater or group of actors or dancers. She could certainly explore the University of North Carolina. The university would have professors and teachers in the arts. Dancing and acting had to be offered. In fact, there were probably productions that might need a talented singer. Cori hadn't explored that avenue yet.

The manager hadn't mentioned money either.

Hope noticed that. She had thought that the manager would want to tout the possible earnings. In fact, she hadn't talked about money for the tryout. Would Disney pony up some funds for Cori's travel? Hope had no idea what was standard and what was negotiable. She felt useless. The world Cori was brushing against was totally new and unexplored. Hope wasn't the guide of choice. Her daughter needed someone better versed in what was standard. Hope didn't want to fail her, but she was adrift at sea.

"What did my manager say?" Cori asked, as soon as she slid into the SUV. "Can I go?"

"I'll tell you the truth," Hope said. "I don't know yet if you'll be trying out or not. Did you know you need acting and dance lessons?"

"She sort of said something about that."

"Sort of? Did you give any thought as to how you're going to manage those lessons, how you're going to pay for them?"

A frown formed over Cori's face. "I thought you'd pay for them."

"If you get a job that pays enough, you may not have time for the lessons."

"You'll help, won't you?"

"You really want to do this, don't you?"

"If you were me, wouldn't you want to?"

"Yes, yes, I would. So, here's what you do. You're going to call Norrie and you're going to ask her about dancing and acting lessons. Then, you're going to call UNCW and ask them about classes and instructors. You can go online, too. You'll probably find some leads there. Make sure to get prices. And don't agree to anything before we talk."

"Roger that." Cori grinned. "I'm gonna do this, I really am."

Hope wasn't home ten minutes before her phone chirped.

It was Detective Robinson.

8

"Hope, I wanted to bring you up to speed concerning the death of Gerald Pantini. It appears he died of a fentanyl overdose. Since he was not a known user, we checked the pills on his desk. It would seem someone replaced his regular prescription with fentanyl pills."

"So, we're talking murder now?"

"I wouldn't think he would commit suicide by swapping pills. That's an extra step a man like him wouldn't take."

"I agree. That also makes the suicide note fake."

"It does. Although, since the note is undated and unsigned Gerald could have written it some time ago."

"The killer might have found the note and left it on the desk to throw you off the track."

"It would seem that way."

"All right, so who did it?"

The detective laughed. "I was about to ask you that question. Any suggestions?"

"I suppose you'll have to start with Gerald's client list. Oh, the wife is the primary suspect, of course. Any idea about the amount of life insurance he carried?"

"None so far. It wasn't important before. We have to look for the people who stand to get the most from the murder."

"Unless it's a revenge murder or envy murder or crazy-no-reason murder," Hope suggested.

"Motives are difficult at best. I'll keep you informed."

Max was dressed as a movie denizen of Mumbai. Hope guessed the residents of Mumbai wore blue jeans and tees, like the rest of the world. Still, she had to admire Max's flair. He wasn't in his chair but dancing around in some sort of jig that looked more

Irish than Indian. She wondered where Max found the energy.

"You look happy. Did you win the lottery?" Hope asked.

"No, no, nothing like that. I worked out the plot for my mystery novel. In keeping with the genre, I have fashioned a number of red herrings that should baffle the reader—until they work out the clues."

"I can't wait. Are you using any characters I know?"

"They say you should write what you know, so my dear Mrs. Herring, you and Cori will be prominently featured in my story."

"I'm not so sure that's a good idea."

"Of course, it is. Mainly because I will move you to the last century, the twenties to be exact."

"The roaring twenties? I'll be a flapper?"

"I hadn't thought of that, but yes, I can make you a flapper. Everyone will underestimate your unique abilities because you don't seem the serious sort."

Hope smiled. "Sounds like you're going to employ a lot of misdirection."

"As much as I can get away with. Whose viewpoint should I use? Or should I use various viewpoints?"

"Well, I think the classic writers used a single

viewpoint, although not necessarily written in first person."

"What exactly does that mean?"

"Well, it means that all the events are seen through the eye of a single character. That character describes the event and offers an explanation of its importance. That character might be wrong, which is another way to send the reader down a different path."

"I see. The detective can misinterpret a clue, and the reader is apt to accept that, correct?"

"Yes, or the detective glosses over a vitally important clue. Again, shaping the reader's evaluation."

"And, if I use multiple points of view?"

"That would add another dimension in confusion. Different characters would offer different opinions. That's not easy to do, because you have to write from that character's persona with different words, different cadence, different emphasis. Not every writer can do that."

Max's face lit up. "Sounds like a bloody good challenge."

"It is. I would recommend that you don't write from the killer's viewpoint. The reader might feel cheated, if the killer pretends to think about something other than the murder."

"Ah, yes. I understand. The killer might well work to get rid of clues which would give away the game."

"Like I said, it's not easy."

"I will take your advice. My detective will provide the clues and the meaning of the clues, although she won't always get it right."

"That's true to form. I don't always get the significance of a case's clues."

"One more question. When the detective figures it all out, does he reveal it?"

"In most novels, the detective does the reveal, but he has to get the murderer to admit it. So, there can't be a premature reveal or if there is, it's wrong."

"Oooh, I do like that. Feed the reader the wrong stew. Lovely."

"Use that in your book. Your readers will love it."

"I will make a note of it. I shall leave you to your work, Mrs. Herring. Cori is downstairs?"

"She is. I think she's trying to figure out how we can afford dance and acting lessons."

"I imagine such lessons are expensive."

"I don't know...yet."

Max faded to nothing, and Hope fired up her computer. She had school chores to tend to, and she wanted to perform a cursory search for the lessons

Cori needed. She guessed the cost would be per hour, like an attorney. Those bills could add up in a hurry.

"What am I thinking?" she whispered to herself. "I should have my head examined."

She didn't answer herself out loud, as she considered answering a sign of a mental issue. As if she needed that. Hope chuckled. She did have her own ghost. If she told anyone about Max, they'd definitely think she wasn't firing on all cylinders.

It took Cori two days to put together a list of possible dance and acting coaches nearby to Castle Park. Norrie helped, although she hadn't heard of most of the coaches, as they were not in her age bracket.

"I looked up their web pages and copied out what I thought was important," Cori said over dinner. "I highlighted the ones I thought might be the best, but I don't know for sure. You can go to their sites and read their resumes."

"They all sound good on paper, don't they?"

"Yeah, but that's what Norrie calls hype. She says some of them will flat out lie."

"That doesn't surprise me. I mean, who's going to go to the trouble of checking educational achievements and former jobs? That's a lot of work. Did you check any reviews that were posted?"

"I didn't have time. Are you going to do that?"

"I think it would be a good idea to read reviews for the people you're thinking of hiring."

"I will. I'll see how many stars they get."

"Remember you have schoolwork to do, too. Researching coaches can't affect your grades."

"I know, I know, it's crazy. Sometimes, I wonder if all this work is worth it. I ask myself if it wouldn't be better to quit school and try to get that job with Disney."

"Not gonna happen, Cori. I know what you're thinking. You can go back to school any time and finish later. People do it all the time except they don't do it all the time. They mean to, they want to, but they don't."

"I'm not an athlete, Mom. I'm not going to lose all the money I make or start doing drugs, or end up with a bunch of people hanging out with me, some sort of posse."

"I know I sound like a downer. I can hear myself. I'm the person who doesn't believe in you, who doesn't think you're good enough. That's not me, Cori. I want you to go after this. Who wouldn't want what you might get. I would. At the same time, I'm your mother. I have to do what's best for you. I have to make sure you're equipped with the skills and knowledge that will get you through your life."

"I'll get that, Mom, I promise."

"I know. Please forgive your mother for being afraid. That's what parents always feel … afraid. I'm going to trust you. If you say you can research coaches and do your schoolwork, I'll believe you."

Cori smiled, and Hope felt better. She hoped she hadn't made a huge mistake. Were parents supposed to trust their teenagers? Was Cori actually able to make good decisions? Had her brain matured enough? Hadn't Hope read that adolescent minds hadn't grown enough? Deferring to a youngster was the height of folly, wasn't it?

She shook her head. She wasn't going to second guess herself … not yet. She was going to trust and verify and work through whatever problems Cori encountered. It was that simple.

They would muddle through.

When Saturday arrived, Hope slipped into the Butter Up Bakery to turn out the cakes and cookies Edsel, the owner, needed. Hope was up to the elbows in white flour, when Detective Robinson walked in.

"This place always smells like Heaven," the detective said.

"I suppose you're right. Heaven should smell good enough to eat."

"Ain't that the truth. You just keep baking and I'll fill you in on what I know so far."

"Great. Try a cookie."

Derrick bit into a big chocolate chip cookie. "You got that right."

He pulled out his notebook and opened it before he grabbed another chocolate chip cookie off the tray.

"I'll start with Gerald's wife. Oh, wait, let me set this up a little. Since the fentanyl pills replaced the regular pills in his bottle, it's difficult to tell exactly when that happened. It looks like Gerald used a new bottle, one filled with the pills that would kill him. His normal dosage was two pills. According to the medical examiner, one poison pill would have been enough. Gerald didn't have a chance. He was alone when he took the pills. Time of death was approximately 9pm. Like I said, the pills might have been in the bottle for a day, a week, or a month."

"Any way to trace the pills?"

"Nope. They're the stuff sold on the street. They're supposed to be cut with something before they're sniffed or smoked or however the user prefers their poison."

"All right, go on."

"His wife, Darlene, found Gerald. He was in their house. She had moved out some months ago. Apparently, there was more than a little bad blood between them. She had come to his office, where they got into some loud arguments, according to Gerald's receptionist. Darlene accused Gerald of holding back the money he promised to provide. She had rent to pay and food to buy, and she wanted to go on vacation in Charlotte. Gerald said he didn't have the money, because his clients were behind in their payments. Gerald was pretty miserly, according to the receptionist."

"Any life insurance?"

"I checked with Gerald's agent. Gerald has some hefty policies that are paid up. Several million dollars are coming to Darlene in the near future. That's above and beyond the value of the business. I have no idea what that might be worth. Probably not a lot without Gerald around to help someone new handle the duties."

"Darlene's debts?"

"The usual raft of credit card debt. It seems Gerald was a penny pincher, so when Darlene danced out the door, she went on a binge. The receptionist did say that several collection agencies had contacted Gerald looking for payments. Gerald told them to go pound sand."

"Did Darlene know about Gerald's meds?"

"Yes, and she did say that the fentanyl pills that were in the bottle were a slightly different color than the ones Gerald usually took. Gerald, however, was largely color blind. He wasn't going to notice."

Hope said, "Darlene hits all the right notes. She needs money. She has access to the house and the pills. She isn't exactly in love with her estranged husband. She had a fight with him that was overheard. Generally, such talk is just angry hot air. In this case, I don't know. Does Darlene have a history of violence?"

The detective smiled. "You always know where to go next, don't you?"

9

Derrick said, "Darlene is not the serene person she might like to be. Not where Gerald was concerned. I've uncovered several incidents where she and Gerald yelled at each other in public. Well, to tell the truth, she did most of the yelling. Gerald was the passive-aggressive type. He would fight dirty, if you know what I mean. According to Darlene, he was the king of dirty tricks."

The timer buzzed and Hope went to the oven to check the cakes. "Do you think Darlene became angry enough to poison Gerald?"

"I would think the angry part would be easy to prove, however, she seemed genuinely surprised by the life insurance. She knew he had some, but she didn't know how much. I checked with the agent, and he said he was under strict orders not to tell her."

"Sounds like Gerald had the idea that Darlene could not be trusted." Hope slid the cakes out of the oven.

"Money is the primary driver in a lot of crimes," Derrick pointed out.

"I'm guessing she'd have no problem finding a note that indicated suicide. She might have written it herself."

"She claims she'd never seen such a note. Her prints weren't on the page. Gerald's were."

"So, the note is probably genuine, but it might have referred to something else. Suicide isn't mentioned in the note."

Derrick cleared his throat. "Then, there's the bar fight."

Hope stared at the detective. "Darlene?"

Derrick nodded. "It wasn't with Gerald. Like I said, he was passive-aggressive. He didn't throw punches. She did."

"I never heard of a woman getting into a bar fight around here."

"That's because it didn't happen in Castle Park or Wilmington. It happened in Charlotte. Darlene was there with a friend for a 'girls' weekend. They went out. She had one too many and got loud. A woman at the bar told Darlene to pipe down, and that was all it took. Darlene threw the first punch, and the second, and the third. She was arrested and spent the night in jail. The charges were dropped when the other woman decided not to pursue anything. I found the arrest when I did a background check. Nothing more than a tavern brawl, but it speaks to her volatile nature."

"But poison is not a volatile murder."

"No, it's not, but Darlene demonstrated a willingness to hurt someone."

The cooling cakes appeared perfect, still, Hope moved them about before she closed the oven and reset the timer. The problem with most ovens was the uneven heating. Moving the cakes was a necessity.

"Were Darlene's fingerprints on the prescription bottle?"

"No. Again, only Gerald's prints were found."

"I suppose if you were going to spike the bottle, you'd wear gloves. Everyone knows that."

"That's what I have so far."

"No other suspects?" Hope wiped her hands on a towel.

"Gerald's brother. He lives in Richmond,

Virginia. I haven't done a deep dive on Harold, but he's the opposite of Gerald. He's in debt up to his elbows and needs money. He has two ex-wives and half a dozen kids. He's behind on his payments. According to Darlene, Harold made several trips here to see his brother. He borrowed some money, but Gerald was no fool. If Harold wasn't going to pay back the loans, Gerald wasn't going to give the brother much."

"Why would Harold kill the cash cow?" Hope asked.

"There's bad blood between the brothers. Darlene thinks Gerald told his brother there might be more money later, when he sold his business. I haven't verified that with Harold. If true, it gives Harold a motive."

"Harold doesn't sound much like a guy who would use poison."

"Not until you read his rap sheet. He's been arrested twice for possession of weed and pills."

"Fentanyl?"

"No, but he knew how to buy drugs. That's half the battle."

"I guess knocking off a loved one isn't so hard after all."

"I have two other possibilities. Boris Green

worked as a physician's assistant in a local partnership, but Boris is a fake. He bought a set of credentials and managed to get hired. By all accounts, he was competent in what he did. The partnership did vet him, and his license checked out. Gerald discovered the problem when he filed with the IRS. It seems the real Boris Green died a few years ago. Someone harvested the documents and sold them to Boris."

"Do you have him in custody?"

"He's not in jail, but he wears an ankle monitor. We know where he is at all times. I haven't talked to him about the murder, but I think he would have access to the pills. When I do chat with him, I may have to put him in a cell. He looks to me like a huge flight risk."

"The feds can't identify him? They can't find his true identity?"

"They think he's Romanian or Polish, and he came across from Mexico. There's no record of that though. I'm trying to get as much as I can, before I bring him in."

"I understand. Your other suspect?"

"Rowdy Sherman. His real name is Ronald Sherman. He's a local. He works for a heating-air conditioning company here in Castle Park. He's a technician. A few years ago, his son was playing backyard football and got a concussion. The doctors who treated him missed a small bubble in a cat scan. The bubble came from a crack in the kid's skull. A germ wiggled through the crack and infected his spinal fluid. Meningitis. The Shermans thought it was the flu. By the time they got him to the hospital, the kid was half brain dead. He died. They sued the doctors and the practice and the hospital. They sued everyone. Gerald provided the numbers for the doctors. According to Rowdy, Gerald made it look like the physicians didn't have much money. So, Rowdy's haul wasn't what he thought he should get. Rowdy blamed the docs. The docs fingered Gerald. Rowdy became very bitter. He lost his son and his money, his wife too, since no woman wants a bitter husband."

"That's awful."

"It is. Rowdy likes to drink, and when he does, he says he's gonna get even with that 'effing bean counter.' Maybe he did."

"Lots of motive, but I don't see how Rowdy found the pills and managed to get them into Gerald's pill bottle."

"Rowdy never worked on the HVAC system at Gerald's house or business, but the company does the maintenance on both. I don't think it would be particularly difficult for Rowdy to get inside the buildings."

Hope picked up a cookie and munched.

"That's it so far," Detective Robinson said.

"Not quite all. Have you talked to Pamela Callier?"

"The doctor? Not yet."

"As I told you the other day, it seems someone was scamming the partnership, paying fake vendors. Her signature was on the checks. Gerald had found the theft and was grilling Pamela. She's worried she's going to be suspected in Gerald's death."

Hope told the detective all she knew about Pamela and the embezzlement. He took notes, listening.

"You'll need to talk to her sooner than later," Hope finished.

"I will."

"I'm not convinced she killed Gerald, even though she fits. I could be wrong. We need more information."

"I understand. I don't need the extra work, but I'm glad you reminded me about her. I have to get going. There is still a lot of work to do. Thanks for the cookies. You'll put your brain to work?"

"I will. We have a crowded field. They all have motive and opportunity since we don't know when someone tampered with the bottle."

"It definitely makes it more difficult. Keep in touch."

The detective left and Hope returned to her baking. As she worked, she considered the list of suspects. Who was innocent? Who was guilty? She asked herself if a team had committed the murder, but that didn't seem likely. There weren't any obvious connections, with the exception of Darlene and Harold, the wife and the brother. Had they conspired to kill Gerald?

Hope didn't see it.

At home, she found Cori practicing her singing. The drills she did seemed odd to Hope, but they did seem to help. Cori didn't slur her words at all, not even when she talked. A benefit of training lips, teeth, and vocal cords.

Max was hunched over his computer, typing away while Bijou was asleep in a chair. The ghost hadn't changed clothes, and Hope knew Max had taken to the Mumbai costume. He stopped and looked back at her.

"Mrs. Herring, I have made the most delightful discoveries. Did you know that you can go online and find any number of helpful forms. There are character development forms and story building forms and outlines, templates, maps, and so many other forms. I chose a story building form and a character-building form. The character form asks for more data than I would include in the story, and I suppose that's all right. The author should know more about his characters than the reader does."

"If they're helpful, then they're worth the effort to fill them out."

"I always thought that a good writer simply sat down and let his mind create. That's not how it works, it would appear. Did you know there are calendars for novel writing also? You put notes, scenes, and action into the boxes. Then, when you get to that day, you know what to write. Marvelous."

Hope said, "In a long story, no one is able to remember the details of all the characters and locations. If the author doesn't take the time to organize the story, he'll be forever fishing through what he's already written to find the proper name and hair color."

Max laughed. "I believe that is true. I can't imagine having to write a tome like *War and Peace* without some sort of outlined detail sheet."

"Famous writers often employ aides that keep

the details straight. They keep what's called a bible. The bible holds all the info they need to edit the daily output of the author."

"I cannot afford an aide."

"Few beginning writers can so they fill out the forms themselves. The forms act like the aides. Also, word processing programs are marvelous at finding words and phrases. So, if you can't remember if you spelled Allison with one 'L' or two, you can search for what you did before. Consistency is important as you write. I have to believe that readers will find every few discrepancies in your writing. When they do, they'll send you a text or email, pointing out your error. Maddening, but helpful for writers, and fun for readers."

"I shall remember that. Perhaps I will purposefully add an error or two, so that the readers will pay attention." Max winked.

Hope laughed. "I'm almost certain some writers have done that. It's a bit of a trick, but it does produce feedback."

"Excellent. Just to let you know, Cori has been at her singing and her computer all day. She's not working too hard, is she?"

"I don't think so. We'll go to dinner tonight to

take her mind off her career … her would-be career. Were you ever a prodigy, Max?"

"Me? I'm afraid not. Perfectly average, if you were to check. Above average, really. I performed good enough to graduate high school and, I always tried to improve my mental abilities. Math, geography, philosophy, writing, I worked on my skill set. Oh, logic too. I enjoyed Sherlock Holmes very much. He possessed a logical mind that I much admired. Oh, I know he was simply someone's concoction, but that didn't matter. He was precise and dogged. He would not give up on a case, no matter how difficult. And, he never got lucky, if you know what I mean. He worked out the solution and solved the case."

"I think he was blessed with criminals who also acted logically. That's a great advantage. You can be very logic driven, but if your thug does things on a whim, it's hard to figure things out. Flip a coin."

Max nodded. "Great idea, Mrs. Herring. I shall create a logical detective who must match wits with a genius who refuses to use logic in his crimes."

"How will the detective win?"

Max laughed. "Perhaps, he won't."

Cori appeared in the doorway. "Hey, Mom, Norrie called."

10

"What did Norrie want?" Hope asked.

"She said I should check with my manager before I start lessons. Norrie thinks that if I get the Disney gig, they'll hire coaches for me. After all, I'm an investment and they want me to get better."

"That makes sense. I'll call your manager and float that past her. Who knows, you might get your training paid for."

"Thanks, Mom."

Cori disappeared and Hope turned to Max. "What do you think?"

"I think I should keep my thoughts to myself," Max answered, "but, we both know I can't do that. For my money, Mrs. Herring, I think you must tread lightly here. I would not wish to be the person someone might blame when things don't go as planned."

"And things don't always go as planned, do they?"

"Not often."

"Wise advice, Max. Thanks."

"You're welcome. I think I need a deerstalker hat, a la Sherlock."

Hope laughed.

Cori's manager did agree that any contract between Cori and Disney would have to include money for acting and dancing lessons. That little fact helped Hope to decide in favor of Cori's audition. In fact, she was in no position to keep Cori from trying out. Holding her back would only make her daughter resentful. Hope anticipated enough teenage blowups. She didn't need to create more. She left it to the manager to set a date, preferably over a weekend. Hope didn't think an audition would take all that much time.

Hope was walking to her car after school when a woman approached. She was roughly Hope's age, but she was dressed like a teenager with cutoff jeans, tank top, sandals, and sunglasses. The tank top put a number of tattoos on display, colorful tattoos on slightly sagging skin. The tattoos complemented the azure blue streaks in the woman's long hair. Hope was reminded of a hippie.

"Hello," the woman said, "I'm Darlene Pantini. You're Hope Herring, right?"

"I am."

"Yeah, great, hey, got a minute? I just came from the station, and, well, everyone around here thinks you're the greatest detective since Houdini."

Hope could have told Darlene that Houdini was not a detective, but that might force her to explain exactly who Houdini was.

"What can I do for you?" Hope asked.

"I'm Gerald's wife, well, separated wife. I thought he committed suicide, but the police say it's murder. I'm smart enough to realize that I'm a suspect. It's always the spouse, right? I mean, I watch enough Netflix and Amazon Prime to know that they always go after the spouse. I need to talk to someone about that."

Hope was straightforward. "Did you kill your husband?"

"No, heck no, I didn't much like him anymore, but I wasn't about to kill him. I won't lie. I considered hurting him. He made me beg for money he was supposed to just give me. The court order, right? He didn't give a flying whatever about any court order.

He just held onto the money and doled it out like it was gold or something. I didn't like begging, but I sure didn't kill him."

"Did you know about his insurance policies?"

Darlene's dark eyes narrowed. Hope guessed the woman had seen her fair share of TV dramas.

"I knew he had some policies, but he always said they were small, just enough to bury him. He never showed them to me. He was a real A-hole about that. He didn't used to lie when we were first married."

"You know that if the police discover that you knew about the insurance money, they'll look very hard at any alibi you offer."

Darlene opened a large, faux leather purse and pulled out a pack of cigarettes, which she offered to Hope.

"No thanks," Hope said.

"They're going to pry into me anyway," Darlene said, as she lit a long, narrow cigarette. "He died of a drug overdose, didn't he?"

"What did the police say?"

"Fentanyl. That's what they said. They wanted to know if I ever did drugs, or if I knew someone who sold the stuff."

"Do you use drugs?"

"Some weed, some alcohol. I've done some speed

too, but I don't mess with cocaine or fentanyl. It all comes from overseas, and those guys don't mind if you die from it."

"I wouldn't know. Did your husband use drugs?"

"Gerald? Come on, the bean counter never got past a light beer and an occasional shot of bourbon. He always said he had to protect his brain because he had all these numbers up there. Everybody's secrets were inside his mind. If he got loose lips, he could cause all sorts of problems."

"How long have you two been apart?"

"A few months. If you want to know why, I can give you all the gory details."

"I'll settle for the short version," Hope told her.

"It won't take long. I'm more than a couple years younger than Gerald. He found me on a tobacco farm out in the country. My father hired Gerald because my father had gotten into trouble with the IRS. My mother was very strict and she scared the bejesus out of both of us. So, when Gerald offered to take me away, I jumped at the chance. Only, I had to marry Gerald first. My father didn't go for shacking up, as he put it. Gerry wasn't much better than my parents. He didn't let me do much. When I started taking some courses at the community college, I found out there was another way to live.

That was the start of it all. I changed. He didn't. I decided I needed to find my true self. I'd been living someone else's life, not my own. He didn't like it, but I was stronger by then. I was leaving, end of story."

"So marrying Gerald was a way off the farm for you?"

Darlene shrugged. "I guess so. I mean, I never really loved him. I thought I did, but I didn't. My girlfriends figured that out. I was just trying to escape."

"Slipping him some fentanyl wasn't part of the escape?"

"No, oh god, no. I would never do that."

Hope studied Darlene a moment. "So, why are you telling me this? What do you want from me?"

"I want you to find Gerry's killer. I mean that. You have to find him."

"Because the insurance company won't pay if they think you did it?"

Darlene rolled her eyes. "Yeah, that's part of it. As long as they aren't sure, they're going to hang onto the money."

"Seems like a wise move for them to do that."

"So, you have to help me. I know you can do it. Everyone says you're the best detective in the world."

"The world is a big place. I'll do what I can. Of

course, you realize that I'll have to investigate you too."

"Me? Why me? I didn't have anything to do with his death." Darlene shook her head. "Oh, right, I'm going to be a suspect forever."

"Until the case is solved."

"Yeah, yeah, I get it. If I give you my number, will you call when you've found the murderer?"

Hope nodded. "The police will have to announce it before I can call you."

"I get it. All right. You got a pen and paper?"

Hope pulled a small notebook and pen from her purse. "Here you go."

"Thanks, thanks a lot. Hey, can I give you a reward or something?"

"I don't accept rewards. If you want to do something with your windfall, donate some of it to the school library. We always need books."

"Great, sure, I can do that."

Hope watched Darlene cross the lot and was pretty sure the woman wasn't about to make a donation or pay a reward. She would probably spend the money on more tattoos.

At home, Hope fixed dinner while Cori practiced her voice lessons and keyboard work. Max was in the attic office, typing away. At least, she assumed he was still working on his murder mystery. When the doorbell rang, she and Bijou headed for the front door where Hope glanced through the peephole and saw a man she didn't recognize. She opened the door, praying that he wasn't some sort of salesman. Bijou stared at him with an unfriendly look on her face.

"Can I help you?"

"You're Hope Herring?"

She nodded.

"My name is Harold Pantini and I'm here to tell you that Darlene did it."

Hope forced a smile. "You're talking about the death of Gerald Pantini?"

"I am. He is ... was my brother. I want justice for him. I think it's damned obvious that his hateful wife killed him."

"Come in, Mr. Pantini. You can tell me how you know this."

Bijou stepped back but kept her eyes pinned on the man.

Harold was tall, taller than his brother. Skinny, his cheeks were hollow, his brownish hair lackluster. Hope thought she spotted a hint of yellowing in his gray eyes, which led her to suspect jaundice. The man had a few of the hallmarks of an alcoholic. His suit hung on him and his shoes needed a good shine.

Yellowed fingers on his right hand shouted "smoker." He didn't look successful. He looked stressed.

"Can I get you something?" Hope asked.

She noticed how his eyes brightened, and she guessed he was ready for a beer—or something stronger. Yet, he shook his head.

"No, no, I can't stay long. I got a long drive back to Raleigh. Looks like it might rain too. It always looks like rain here. I get so sick of it. Rain is depressing. There is no denying that. I hate it. I wish I didn't, but I do. One of these days, I'm going to pack up and move to Arizona. Sun every day. That suits me. I don't care how hot it gets. I just want to wake up to sunlight."

"I think variety is the key to a healthy mind. If you see the same thing every day, you'll soon feel blue."

"Not me, not with the sun, but that's another story. I'm here to tell you why it was Darlene who killed my brother."

Bijou let out a little hiss.

"What's wrong with the cat?" the man asked.

Hope ignored the question. "Go ahead with what you were going to say, Mr. Pantini."

"You ever met Darlene?"

"I have."

"She's a piece of work, ain't she? You see those tattoos, that hair? Did she show you her pierced bellybutton?"

Hope shook her head.

"She must have been on her best behavior with you. Get a drink or two in her, and she'll show you her whole kit and kaboodle. That's a fact. That's half the reason Gerry dumped her."

"She said she left him."

"What would you expect her to say? No, it was him. He tossed her fat butt out of the house and filed for divorce."

"Are you sure about that?"

"No, no, but he said he was going to. My brother was pretty good about following through with stuff. If he said he was going to divorce her, then he was."

"If he wanted to be rid of her, why is she the beneficiary on his insurance policies?"

Harold's eyes flitted to the side, as if trying to avoid the question. "To my way of thinking, he got too busy. He should have seen to that right off. It's for certain that as soon as Darlene found out, she fed him whatever it was that killed him."

"It was fentanyl, he died of an overdose."

"Because she gave it to him. She got it from one

of those druggies she hangs out with. You would not believe the riffraff she runs with."

"You're certain? She told me she had no idea she was on the life insurance policies."

"That's a lie. She knew all about it. I know because I was there when Gerry told her. He wanted me and her to know."

"When was this?"

"Just a month before he died. He told her he was taking her off the policies, and he wanted me to be a witness. He didn't want to have to go to court. Don't let Darlene fool you. She looks as dumb as soleless shoes, but she can spot a sucker when she sees one."

Hope nodded, unwilling to give much credence to Harold's version of events.

"So, you're saying she killed Gerald in order to get the insurance?"

"Absolutely. Gerry had already changed his will, so I would get his business after he died."

"You're an accountant?"

"No, no, he had all the brains for numbers. He wanted me to sell the business."

"You're telling me you had a reason to kill your brother?"

"Sure, maybe, but why would I do that? Gerry alive was going to get richer and richer. I could wait."

Hope wasn't at all sure that Harold could wait for his ship to arrive. He looked but a month or two short of the street.

"I'm glad you stopped by," Hope said. "Do you have a copy of the will?"

"I don't. I'm guessing it's still in his home office. That's where he showed it to me. The police will come across it soon enough ... if Darlene don't find it and burn it."

"I'm guessing your brother's attorney will have a copy."

Harold's face brightened. "I think you're absolutely correct. I gotta call him, but not tonight. I have to get going."

"If you get a chance, call Detective Robinson with the police and tell him what you told me."

"I can do that. I will, although people say you're the one that finds all the killers."

"I assure you that's not true."

A few words more and Hope was able to guide Harold out the door. She had no sooner closed the door when Cori ran into the room, phone in hand.

"She wants to talk to you," Cori said.

"Who?"

"The casting director at Disney."

11

Hope thought the casting director sounded perfectly normal and accommodating. Yes, she could schedule the audition for a weekend so Cori would not miss any school. Fly in on a Friday night, stay close to the Disney property, and fly out on Sunday. It all sounded so matter of fact, but Hope knew the trip would be stressful for her and Cori. It was like trying out for the U.S. Olympic team. How could Cori guarantee that her voice would be pitch perfect for the audition?

Norrie.

Hope would have to pick Norrie's brain for audition tips. Certainly, there were time-tested methods for insuring against failure. Practice was certainly part of the prep, but there were things Hope couldn't know about. Although excited when the call ended, Hope was afraid also. Cori, a neophyte, would be auditioning against children who had been acting since birth. Well, that was a bit over the top, but certainly, most of the singers would have more experience than Cori. That couldn't be helped.

Hope and Cori would have to accept whatever happened.

"Am I going?" Cori asked when Hope stepped into the teen's bedroom.

"Of course, you're going. We're going together."

"Yippee!" Cori jumped out of her chair and hugged Hope. "Thank you, thank you, thank you."

"Don't thank me yet. We're not even on the plane. There's work to be done."

"I'm practicing really hard."

"It's not just practice. You have to talk to Norrie. I mean really talk to her. She knows about auditioning. She'll be able to give you some important tips."

"Roger that. She'll give me good advice. She wants me to succeed."

"I'm sure she will."

Hope was on her lunch break the next day, when Detective Robinson called.

"What are you doing after school?" the detective asked.

"Taking Cori to her singing lesson and then fixing dinner, why?"

"If I bring pizza for dinner, will you take a ride with me. There's a person of interest I want to question about the Gerald Pantini case."

"I don't see why not. Will it take long?"

"No, I don't think so. I just need someone to help evaluate this guy."

"Guy?"

"Name's Rowdy Sherman. He has been known to make threats."

"About Gerald?"

"Among others. He can be hard to handle, but I think he'll be a bit subdued if a woman is there, especially someone like you."

"Me? Why am I different?"

"You solve murders. That might make him a bit more leery."

"Fair enough. Pepperoni and mushroom, that's what Cori and I like."

The detective laughed.

Rowdy lived in Shady Acres, a trailer park a mile outside Castle Park. Trailers and mobile homes were reasonably cheap in North Carolina and small communities dotted the rural countryside. The Acres, as it was called, was typical, consisting of some very well-kept trailers alongside trailers that needed more than a little work. The homes with children were the ones with toys in the yard. Space was always a consideration with a trailer, especially with kids involved. Unless there was some sort of storage shed included, the toys sat outside.

There were no toys outside the rusted trailer that faced Hope. There were exactly seven Keep Out and No Trespassing signs in front. Hope looked for signs of a dog, but she didn't spot one.

"Friendly man, isn't he?" Hope said.

"Hardly," Detective Robinson said. "Rowdy is an engine mechanic, when he's working. I've heard that he can work wonders with an internal combustion engine, but he has the social graces of a hog, rough around the edges."

"What do I need to know about him?"

"First thing is he has a beef with the doctors that Gerald Pantini worked for."

"What kind of beef?"

"Medical malpractice. Rowdy's son, Rowdy Junior, fell off his bike. That was the official take, although I know of at least one doc that thinks he was beaned on the head by his father. Rowdy Senior likes to use his fists sometimes. Anyway, Rowdy Junior went to the hospital and had a CAT scan.

Nothing showed up, nothing the technician or doctor could see. Rowdy Junior went home and two months later, he came down with what looked like the flu. Fever, vomiting, headache, the usual symptoms. Rowdy called his doc, who was part of the group that Pamela belongs to. The doctor said it was flu. If he wasn't better in twenty-four hours, bring in the boy. Fair enough."

The detective went on. "A day later, Rowdy Junior was convulsing. He didn't have the flu. He had meningitis. By the time they started treatments, he was in bad shape. But, they saved him. He lost his hearing and eyesight, but he was alive. Six months later, Rowdy Junior does a repeat. Same symptoms. The doc was certain that it was the flu this time, since Junior had already had meningitis. Rowdy brought in the boy, and the boy was touch and go. Well, two bouts of meningitis six months apart on a healthy kid isn't common. So, they go back and look at the CAT scan again. This time, they spotted a small crack in the skull, behind the right eye. It was small, but bacteria are way smaller. They couldn't save Junior this time. Rowdy went off the deep end for a while. Then, he got a lawyer and went after the hospital, docs, techs, anyone and everyone. Rowdy figured he'd be living on cloud nine, but it doesn't work that way. Junior was a kid, whose future earnings were unknown. Rowdy signed the usual waivers, which limited what he could claim. Instead of a million, he got less than a hundred thousand, which he had to split with his attorney. Rowdy became one bitter, bitter man. He claimed Gerald hid a bunch of money for the doctors somehow, so there wasn't much of a pot to raid. Everyone colluded to keep Rowdy poor. You're going to hear that claim. I just want you to be aware."

"It sounds as if he was dealt a really bad hand," Hope said.

Derrick frowned. "Not if he caused the fracture in the first place."

Detective Robinson's knock on the door wasn't answered right away. Hope had the feeling that whoever was inside wanted her and the detective to stew for a minute or two. When the door opened, she faced a bearded man with bloodshot eyes. His light brown hair was long and scraggly, his T-shirt stained with something akin to oil, his jeans old and worn. Hope guessed he no longer had a wife.

"What do you want?" Rowdy growled.

"Just to talk," the detective said. "You heard about Gerald Pantini, right?"

"You come to me for that? I didn't have anything

to do with him. Not that I'm sad he's gone. I'm not. He was a cheating son of ... gun. As far as I'm concerned he had every reason to go sideways."

"He didn't kill himself. He was murdered."

Rowdy's face changed slightly. He became more wary. "Now, I see what this is about. Well, I didn't kill him."

"Mind if we ask some questions?" Hope said.

"Who are you? No, wait, I know who you are. You're the woman who catches all the killers, aren't you?"

"Mrs. Herring has helped in the past," the detective said. "And not just with murderers. She's also cleared a lot of people who were accused of murder."

Rowdy looked from face to face. Hope could see his brain working. Would she convict him or clear him?

"Come in," Rowdy said. "I don't have nothing to hide."

Hope passed by Rowdy, as did Robinson. What Hope found inside did not fit the outside. The trailer was remarkably clean and neat. She would not have guessed it.

"I don't think this is going to take long," Rowdy said, "so, you got no reason to sit."

"Fair enough," Robinson said. "Have any idea how Pantini died?"

"I heard it was pills, which would suit a coward like him."

"Fentanyl," Robinson said. "Overdose. Someone filled his pill bottle with fentanyl pills."

"Figures. It wasn't me. I can't find any traction with lying, so I'll repeat what we all know. I threatened Pantini and all the doctors he worked for. They cheated me out of a son and a lot of money. I don't think there's any doubt about that."

"When was the last time you saw Pantini?" Hope asked.

"It's been at least a year. We don't swim in the same pond, if you know what I mean."

"What if I told you that you had been spotted near his office six weeks ago?"

Rowdy rubbed his chin. "He still on Chestnut?"

Robinson nodded.

"Well, I delivered a crappy Kia to a house on Chestnut around that date. I waited on the sidewalk for my ride. I guess that's when someone spotted me."

"You didn't enter his office?"

"Had no need. Oh, I knew he was there. I also knew that if anything happened to him, I'd get a visit from the police, and here you are. You surprised me because I heard it was by his own hand."

"You ever take drugs?" Hope asked.

"Do I look like a user?" Rowdy held out arms with thick veins and several tattoos. "I been clean for two years. I know that doesn't mean I don't know how to get something like fentanyl, but I didn't. Back when my son ... well, I was using then. I said a lot of dumb stuff. Am I sorry that little pencil pusher is dead? No, but I'm not glad he was murdered."

Hope couldn't tell if Rowdy was telling the truth or not.

"Did you cause the crack in your son's skull?" Hope asked.

Rowdy glared, anger flushing his face. Hope thought he might explode into action. She noticed that Robinson had moved his hand to his hip.

"That's a lie," Rowdy hissed. "I can't say I never touched that boy, as I always thought a

swat on the butt was what a boy needed now and again. But I never hit him in the head. I never took a belt or ruler or baseball bat to him. He didn't need that kind of whipping, and I never give it to him."

"How did the lie get started?"

"It was the doctors. When they saw the train coming down the track, they started all manner of rumors. They said I beat my wife and son. They say I cheated folks when I fixed their cars. They say I once cut off a man's nose cause he was staring too hard at my wife. Those are all lies. I got in a fight or two over the years, but I never used a knife or a gun. That kind of damage lands you in jail."

"And the doctors spread lies so people would believe you hit your son?" Hope asked.

"Why else would they do it?"

"Did Pantini tell the same lies?" the detective questioned.

"Not to my face, but then the doctors wouldn't say that to my face either."

"I'm going to need the name of the person who owned that KIA you delivered," Robinson said.

"Yes, sir, give me a minute."

Rowdy disappeared into another room.

"What do you think?" Robinson asked.

"He's certainly capable, and he holds a huge grudge," Hope answered. "But I have to wonder why he would start with Pantini. He was just the accountant. It would seem to me that the doctors would be the prime targets."

"I agree."

Rowdy reappeared and handed a slip of paper to Robinson. "That should be enough. I haven't talked to the owner since I delivered it. I'm not going to make a call when you walk out the door. Like I said, I got nothing to hide."

On the drive back to the house, Hope wondered about a father who had lost a son and never received any sort of fair response. A man like Rowdy Sherman might have the patience to wait years before he struck. How long would someone wait before they exacted revenge? It was hard to judge.

"I think you might want to tell the doctors that Rowdy hasn't forgotten. If Rowdy did murder Gerald, they're all in jeopardy," Hope suggested.

"I let them know already. Oh, by the way, I added Italian sausage to half of a pizza ... for me."

Hope laughed.

In the middle of the meal, Detective Robinson took a call. Ten minutes later, he returned. "Want to meet Boris Green?"

12

Hope looked into the interrogation room and studied the man at the table. The one-way glass protected her from his gaze, which seemed positively bored. That surprised Hope as Boris Green had been hauled in for the murder of Gerald Pantini. Boris wore blue jeans, a polo shirt, and sandals without socks. That was not surprising. In southeastern North Carolina, people often went without socks, even in winter.

"What do you think?" Detective Robinson asked.

"I can't tell," Hope answered. "Do you know who he really is?"

"Not yet. The best I can do is assure you that he is not Boris Green."

Hope made eye contact with Derrick. "Then, let's shake the tree and see what drops to the ground."

"My sentiments exactly."

Through the introductions, Boris eyed Hope. She had the feeling those light brown eyes belonged to a cagey man who was accustomed to gauging people at a moment's notice.

"What's your name?" the detective asked.

"Boris Green," the man answered.

Hope noted that Boris was cuffed, and the cuffs were secured to the table. That made her wonder if he was more dangerous than he looked.

"You know, Boris, you look pretty good for a man who's been dead for five years. Want to try again?" the detective asked.

A sheepish smile spread Boris's face. "How do you know this?"

"The social security number you're using. It belonged to the real Boris. It wasn't hard to discover his death. Did you kill him?"

The grin disappeared. "No, no, I had nothing to do with his death. I just took on his identity."

Derrick leaned back in his chair. "Want to start at the beginning?"

"You're not going to set me free, are you?"

"Sorry, Boris, no can do. Tell me your real name.

I can't keep calling you Boris."

"What is she?" Boris pointed to Hope.

"She is a civilian who helps the police on occasion."

"Ah, yes, the master detective everyone talks about. You're quite famous."

"I'm a schoolteacher," Hope said. "Once in a while, I manage to help the police. That's it."

Boris said, "Let me guess, you're helping the police with the murder of Gerry Pantini."

"The beginning," Detective Robinson prompted. "Start talking."

"Ah, yes, the beginning. Lying now wouldn't help me, would it?"

"You already know the answer to that."

"My real name is Szymon Mazur and I came here from Poland by way of Mexico. I crossed the Rio Grande River four years ago. It was quite easy. No one stopped me. I traveled to New York where I became someone else. Who that was doesn't matter. I got a job in a hospital as an orderly. Hospitals always need people to handle the dirty jobs. I didn't mind. Those jobs were better than what I did in Poland."

"You met the real Boris Green in the hospital."

The man nodded. "He was a good man and he

took me under his wing. A practical nurse with credentials. He was gay, but I didn't mind that. He had his gay people, I had some friends from Warsaw. We lived together and I paid him a modest rent, a pittance really. Then, Boris got sick."

Szymon paused and looked around the room. Hope guessed he was trying to massage the truth to his advantage.

"Go on," the detective prompted.

"Boris taught me very much about being a practical nurse. I knew I could do that job. I just needed a license which would have taken me two years more. Boris was not going to live that long."

"So, you killed him off and stole his identity."

"I had nothing to do with his death," the man told them. "He jumped all by himself."

"He killed himself by jumping? Why?"

"He had no family. I was the brother he should have had. I took care of him, but he was not a brave man. The treatments punished him horribly. He couldn't take it. He wanted to quit, but I persuaded him to keep going."

"Is that when you started planning to become him?"

Szymon shrugged. "It seemed like a good and easy thing to do. We looked alike ... mostly. I got a new driver's card and a passport. I was already paying the bills from his checking account. It seemed that becoming Boris helped us both."

"Until he jumped?"

"That was a surprise. But I was prepared. I buried him with dignity and became him. I moved from New York as soon as I could. I stopped in Philadelphia and Virginia Beach. I liked Virginia Beach, but I thought that was still too close to New York. In America, it is easy to become lost. No one stops you to see your papers, unless you do something wrong. Eventually, I landed here in Castle Park. A licensed practical nurse can usually find a job."

"All right," the detective said. "You landed a job with the doctors' practice. Gerald Pantini handled the finances which meant he paid you, correct?"

"This is true, but I did not kill him."

"You have access to drugs including fentanyl, correct?"

He shrugged. "Many people can buy fentanyl on the street. It is not difficult."

"When did Gerald discover you were a fake?"

"Some months ago. I made the mistake of staying too long in one place."

"Is that why you killed him?"

"I did not do anything to him."

"We're going to find your fingerprints in his office, aren't we?"

Boris shrugged. "I never said I did not talk to him."

"Why didn't you run?" Hope asked.

"I had intended to, but the money was good."

"And you couldn't persuade Gerald to leave you alone, right?"

"I offered him money. He would not take it, but I still did not kill him."

Hope found it impossible to read Szymon. She guessed he had become adept at lying. He had probably learned how at an early age. Moving from country to country and city to city had simply given him the chance to perfect his storytelling.

"Is any of this true?" Hope asked.

Boris shrugged. "Some, the part about me not killing Pantini, that's true. Some of the other stuff ... perhaps not so much."

"Did anyone else know you were not Boris Green?"

"No. Pantini was the only one. He checked the social number carefully."

On the way back to her house, Detective Robinson opened the conversation.

"What's your call?"

"The man is a prolific and accomplished liar," Hope answered. "He's proven that by being able to keep his nursing credentials without ever actually attending classes. I think he's giving us what he thinks we want and holding back a great deal."

"How do you think we can get more?"

"I'm pretty sure we can't, unless we catch him in the act. He's not going to offer anything unless it's to his advantage to do so."

"So, file charges?"

"I don't think so. Well, I think it would be wise to file something and treat him as a flight risk but let him leave jail with an ankle monitor."

"He'll just get rid of it, if it suits him."

"Of course, but that will allow you to file new charges. Also, analyzing his movements might give us important information."

"I don't have the manpower to follow him around town."

"I know, but he's more likely to make a mistake if he's out of custody. And look at it this way. If he really wanted to disappear again, he'd be gone by now. In fact, I think he's still here because there's something to be gained by staying. You might look for an anchor."

"Anchor?"

"Someone or something that keeps him in Castle Park. When a roamer stops roaming, it's usually because he's found a reason to stay put."

"Makes sense. All right, I'll see if I can arrange an electronic monitor. We'll see if it gives him a way to make a mistake."

Hope found Cori in her room with Bijou, but she wasn't singing or playing on the keyboard.

"What's up?" Hope asked.

"Just the normal stuff ... being scared to death."

"By the audition?"

"What else? What if I'm horrible? What if it's a bad day? What if I freeze?"

"Certainly, those things can happen. Everyone has bad days, weak performances. If you focus on that, you won't make it."

"How do I make it?"

"You do what you've been doing. You practice, and you target your practice on the things you don't do so well. People like to practice what they're already good at. Makes sense. It's fun. People who look to the future, practice what they're not so good at. They shore up their weaknesses, not their strengths."

"Won't their strengths suffer if they do that?"

"No, they'll stay strong. When you add more

arrows to your quiver, you enhance your chances of bagging game."

"Yuck. But I understand. Weaknesses, here I come."

Hope found Max lying on the office floor. He wore a deerstalker hat and had a pipe in his mouth, although he wasn't smoking.

"Can ghosts smoke?" Hope asked.

"We can, and the upshot is that it won't affect the lungs we no longer have. Most ghosts don't smoke because it doesn't provide the same stimulus. There is no need."

"Any particular reason you're on the floor?"

"I was reading some Doyle and came upon Sherlock doing odd things. Of course, he was an opium addict, so doing odd things came with the territory. If strange positions helped him, perhaps they could me."

"Stuck on your story?"

"A little. I want a certain thing to happen, and my characters are resisting. I can't get them to do what I want."

"Ah, you've found the writer's curse. Readers think you have complete and total control over the people you create. It's not so, is it?"

"Not in the slightest. Every time I need a character to do what I want, I have to go back in the story and provide some sort of impetus."

Hope said, "If your heroine has to save a drowning child, you should make sure she can swim."

"Precisely. Making them very human also means they must operate within the confines of their lives. The pastor doesn't suddenly become an atomic physicist. The aging doctor doesn't perform as an acrobat in a circus."

"Constraints, Max, people come with constraints. The reader understands that and gets miffed if a character does whatever you want him or her to do. Have you been keeping up on your character summaries?"

"I have, which is why I'm stuck. I can't make the blind man see."

Hope laughed. "You'll figure out something. Every author goes through the same process. It's called thinking. It's difficult, always difficult."

"Which is why so few people know how to truly think."

"I will second that observation, as some of my students can't think well. Someone should invent a thinking pill. Take a dose and immediately think like Sherlock."

"I'd settle for thinking like Doyle. I need to do some considering. Good night, Mrs. Herring."

"Good night, Max. Think well."

He laughed and was gone.

The next morning, Hope was sitting at her desk in her classroom, waiting for the students to arrive. She was surprised when Allison Crush smiled her way into the room. Hope thought that Allison's designer jeans looked new, as did her flowery top.

"Hey," Allison said. "Got a minute?"

"Just one, the buses will be arriving soon."

"I heard that the police picked up one of our nurses. Is that right? Did they grab Boris Green?"

"It is, and I think he's going to be charged with something today."

"What did he do? Can you tell me?"

"He crossed the border illegally."

"You're kidding. Where is he from?"

"Poland. He's been moving about the country for some time."

"Wow, that's something, isn't it? Anything else you can tell me?"

"Why do you need to know?'

"I help Pamela with the managerial duties of our partnership. If Boris is going to be out of the picture for a while, we need to start the recruiting process.

You're probably aware of how long it takes to find a good candidate."

"Luckily, I'm not part of any personnel team."

"I wish I weren't."

"I think you should start looking for someone to replace Boris. If nothing else, he won't qualify for the job he has, despite his experience."

Allison sighed. "Darn it, I was hoping it was something like jaywalking or maybe skipping out on a check. Wait, did Gerry know that Boris was a fake?"

"I can't speak to that. He might have."

"Which would make Boris a suspect. Now, I see. He might be a murderer as well as a liar."

Hope shrugged. "Maybe."

"Oops, I hear the pitter-patter of little feet. Thanks, Hope. I have work to do."

"Don't we all."

For a moment, Hope wondered how Allison knew that the police had picked up Boris. Not that it mattered. News like that traveled on the wind. As students filtered into her room, Hope's phone chimed.

A text.

The casting director wanted to set up the audition.

13

Hope waited until after Cori's singing lesson to tell her and Norrie about the audition. Hope had settled it with the casting director. The plane seats were reserved, even if they weren't first class. That might come later, if Cori made the cast. They had a room just outside the Disney studios. A car and driver would ferry them from the airport to the hotel to the studio. Everything would be arranged. Hope would collect a stipend for meals, which wasn't a lot, but it was something. The first audition would be Saturday morning. If a second one was needed, it would be Saturday evening. The casting director was quite enthusiastic, but then, Hope guessed that she was always enthusiastic. When she filled a slot, everyone was happy.

Cori paled a little at the news, but Norrie took it in stride. She reassured Cori that auditions were the life blood of an entertainer. Even if she didn't get the part, people would remember her when another role popped up. Every audition was a good audition. Cori had to remember that.

"So, it's really going to happen," Cori said on the ride home.

"It is," Hope said. "We'll have a great time."

"I'm scared."

"Of course, you are. So am I. But that's half the fun. Being afraid isn't a bad thing, unless it paralyzes you. Remember that. As long as you're not frozen in place, being afraid is an adrenaline rush. Some people live for that."

"Crazy people."

"Nope, just people who like living on the edge."

"I'm not one of those people."

"No matter how it turns out, you'll be better off for taking the risk. You may not think that now, but you will later. Most people regret not taking a chance."

Max took the news with jovial hurrahs. He told Cori she was going to "knock 'em dead." Cori laughed at that. What singer ever wanted to kill the audience? Max didn't bother to explain. He simply bolstered her mood, which led Cori to ask him to come with them. Max couldn't do that. He had to stay close to the house. Ghost rules.

That night, as Hope sat at her computer doing some schoolwork, she received a call from Detective Robinson.

"What have you got?" Hope asked.

"We managed to get an ankle monitor on Szymon before we cut him loose. We both know those monitors have limited usefulness. I doubt he's going to do something that will give us the killer, but you never know."

"I don't know how sensitive those things are but keep an eye on it. If it sits in one place too long, he's probably no longer wearing it."

"Yeah, I know. We'll do what we can. I've arranged for some units to drive by the house on an irregular basis. We wouldn't want our suspect to get used to every hour on the hour."

"Great. You know, while I understand that he's an accomplished liar and con man, I don't see him as a murderer. Of course, I'm no expert in that realm."

"You should be. You're pretty good at judging people."

"Not me. You know Allison Crush is a psychologist and she's worked with Szymon. You might give her a call and get her input."

"Why don't you do that, Hope? She'll probably open up to you. I think she would be wary with me."

"Perhaps, you're right. I'll do it. Just as soon as I get back from Florida."

"Florida? What's up down there?"

"Cori has an audition with Disney. They want to hear her sing. It's for some sort of streaming show they're doing."

"Let me know how it goes. I want her to do well, but I would hate to lose my best detective."

"I have mixed feelings too, but I'm not going to worry about it. That's a bridge we'll cross when we come to it. You know how it is. Most of the things you fear might happen, never do."

"Amen, Hope, amen to that."

The next morning, Hope called Allison. With a bit of persuasion, the woman agreed to meet Hope for a drink after work. After dropping Cori at home so she could do homework, Hope headed out to the Tar Heel Brewery, a small brewery on the edge of town. Tucked away on a side street, the brewery's industrial chic decor included exposed brick walls, dangling Edison bulbs, reclaimed wood accents, and inviting mismatched vintage couches and over-stuffed armchairs.

Local artwork from up-and-coming artists deco-rated the walls, adding pops of color to the taproom. Behind the bar, the brewing equipment was on display through glass windows so people could watch the brewing process.

On certain nights, there were live music perfor-mances from indie bands. The atmosphere provided the perfect place to relax and unwind with friends. Patrons chatting and laughing mingled with the faint music and clinking of glasses. With its hip vibe and cozy, welcoming decor, the brewery was a popular spot for the locals to hang out and enjoy great craft beer, wine, and mixed drinks in an eclectic setting.

Hope found Allison seated at the bar, sipping a large mug of beer.

"Hey, Hope," Allison said. "What are you drinking?"

"White wine, small glass," Hope answered.

"Gotcha." Allison waved over a heavy bartender who then produced a glass of Chardonnay.

"The beers are really pretty good here," Allison

said. "What can I do for you? I'm guessing this is about our recent murder?"

"It is. How well do you know Boris Green?"

"Not as well as I thought I did."

"Why is that?"

"Well, for one thing, I heard he's wearing a monitor on his ankle which means something is wrong."

"He entered the country illegally and he stole an identity. He's a flight risk."

Allison shook her head. "You know, he had me completely fooled and I pride myself on being able to read people."

Hope said, "He fooled everyone, everywhere he went. Don't feel bad. If it's any consolation, I can't read him either."

Allison gave a slight nod. "So, how can I help?"

"I am trying to decide if he's capable of murder. You know, some people can do it, but a lot of people can't. What's your take on Boris?"

Allison tapped her forehead with a finger, as if thinking. "My gut says no, he's not a killer. I see him as a scammer who will do what it takes to stay in the United States. I don't think he sees a need to kill."

"What if Gerald Pantini threatened to expose

him and turn him over to Federal agents for deportation?"

Allison said, "I think Boris would pack a small bag and catch the first bus to Denver or someplace far away. That's probably what he's done in the past, right? He just moves on."

Hope sipped her wine. "He was involved with a death in the past in New York. He said his roommate committed suicide, but I don't know that for a fact."

"Oh, that's a surprise. If that's the case, then he might have killed Gerry. He probably thought he'd never get caught."

"I was thinking that, but why hang around once he placed the pills?" Hope questioned. "Wouldn't it make more sense to sabotage the pill bottle and then vamoose?"

"I'm not sure. To someone so devious, it might make more sense to stay for a bit as if he had done nothing wrong. The police would be looking for anyone who bolted. That's a sign of guilt."

"You're probably right." Hope looked around the room, thinking.

"Or else, he had something coming to him. You know, some money or something. He would hang around for that even after he killed Gerry. There's a rumor that some money is missing from the partnership accounts. I'm not going to name names, but what if that someone paid Boris to kill Gerry?"

Hope said, "That would bring an extra person into a murder plot, which generally creates a very wobbly situation. Pay someone, and what's to keep them from wanting more?"

"What's to keep the other person from killing off Boris? That's the only way to be certain that he won't turn state's witness."

"That could happen," Hope agreed. "I still don't see Boris killing someone. Better to run and live to fight another day. Since he's on a monitor, we might well see if he's going to go rabbit. I doubt he would want to go to trial."

"Who would?"

By the time Hope reached the house, she had convinced herself that Szymon was not the murdering type. He might kill someone in a fit of rage or self-defense, but the pills pointed to a calculating killer. Szymon didn't fit that role.

Hope made sure to call Detective Robinson and relay her conversation with Allison. The detective wasn't so sure that Szymon wasn't good for the death, but there was little evidence to prove anything at this point. The police were still digging up new information. Szymon was housebound.

Maybe the pressure would get to him. They could only wait.

The flight from Wilmington to Florida was long, mainly because Hope and Cori had to switch planes. Luckily, the in-flight movies provided some distraction. Hope needed a good movie as much as Cori did.

Their driver was a middle-aged man from Turkey. He chatted with them on the way to the hotel. He had a daughter that he called "lazy." She had been born in America and so had learned American ways. She had adopted the lazy life of going to school and living off her parents. He didn't mind helping her—as long as she was willing to work. Borrowing money to spend ten hours a week in an air-conditioned classroom didn't qualify as "work."

Cori rolled her eyes at the little tirade.

A quick dinner at a little Thai restaurant not far from the hotel was followed by a restless night. While Cori seemed to sleep fairly well, Hope tossed and turned all night. In a way, she was more nervous than her daughter. Neither of them ate much breakfast. Cori was following instructions from Norrie. No singer wanted to have a stomach so full it interfered with her breathing. Hope limited her coffee intake. A nervous Nellie didn't need a caffeine push.

A different driver took them to the studio, where they were photographed at the gate. Hope didn't know if the studio used facial recognition. Not that it mattered. She didn't expect to be on the site for very long. They rode a golf cart to an old building where they ended up in the casting director's office. It was small and crammed with scripts and photos. The director herself was a bit older than Hope. Orange and blue hair, long nails, a ring in her nose, the director wasn't what Hope had pictured. Then, she was pretty sure she and Cori didn't fit the director's vision either.

Hope listened to the brief introduction the director made, explaining the process. Hope was more than welcome to stay with Cori, or there was a cafeteria where Hope could hang out. Hope opted for staying with Cori, which seemed to relax everyone. Then, it was on to the actual audition.

"You're familiar with the music?" the director asked.

Cori nodded. "I've been practicing."

"Good. You'll sing that one first. Then, we're going to give you a new song, a different song, one you've never seen before. You read music, correct?"

Cori nodded. Hope noticed the tension in her

daughter's jaw. She hadn't expected something off the cuff.

"Great. We're going to evaluate your ability to take a new song and make it yours. If we're shooting an episode a week, you'll have a new song a week. Not all the songs are original. Some will come from movies or shows. Just so you're aware."

"Cool," Cori said.

"Don't be afraid. I know that's cliché. Everyone is afraid. Do your best."

The audition commenced, and Hope sat to one side. Cori was recorded, as other directors would want to hear her. To Hope's ear, Cori nailed the first song, every note pure and on key. Then, the second song was handed to Cori, who had five minutes to go through it. While Hope thought her daughter aced the second song as she had the first, Hope could tell from the teen's slumping shoulders that Cori didn't agree.

At that point, the director thanked Cori and Hope and sent them back to the hotel. If necessary, Cori might be called back in the evening. Being called back was neither a good thing nor a bad one. Nothing could be inferred from a callback. No matter what, a decision would be made by the end of the next week. There were other girls to test. Cori would be informed. No one was going to ghost her.

"I blew it," Cori said as they walked into the hotel lobby.

"You were great," Hope countered. "They know it, I know it. Let's get some ice cream."

"Yeah."

14

___

When Hope and Cori boarded the plane, there had been no callback, no second chance. Hope took that as a good sign. Cori was not on the chopping block. Whether it was success or failure, it was final. Hope was glad, she didn't like maybes. On the flight back to North Carolina, Cori did homework and caught up on her school reading and Hope took the opportunity to ponder the death of Gerald Pantini. Who had killed him?

The suspects had been questioned once. Since no one knew when the fentanyl had been added to his meds, no particular suspect was fingered. It could have been a day, a week, or a month before the death. There was no way to narrow the time. The police would have to find some other means to pinpoint the killer. She wasn't sure what that might be. They needed a confession. She was certain the actual killer wasn't going to step forward. Why go to the trouble of spiking Gerald's pills if the killer wanted to be known as the killer? That wasn't going to happen.

So, how to solve the case?

To Hope's way of thinking, the killer needed to make a mistake. There had to be a stumble, something that would put the murderer in the spotlight. What that might be? Hope was stumped. She supposed the closest thing to a mistake was Szymon's not leaving town. He must have known that sooner or later his true identity would be revealed. When that happened, he faced deportation. Deportation would mark the end of his dream. He would have to start over again, and the second effort would be more difficult than the first. What did staying put buy him—if he was the killer? Still, he probably had the most to lose. Hope had the feeling that he was holding something back.

What was it?

When Hope landed in Wilmington, she was no closer to that answer. Perhaps, with Detective Robinson's help, they could scare Szymon into a confession.

Not likely.

Hope didn't talk to Cori about the audition or any possible role. She thought it would be better if Cori could push that distraction from her head—until she received the official news. Hope, like her daughter, was half convinced the offer would never come. That provided better ego-armor than believing that Cori would be belting out songs in a Disney show. Hope was pretty sure the teen was not bragging to her classmates. She kept up her scheduled lessons with Norrie and stayed busy with school. Hope was proud of her daughter. When Friday arrived without a word from the casting director, Cori asked if she could spend the night with Lottie, her best friend.

"That's a great idea," Hope said. "You two have fun."

"We will. I think we're going to a movie. You'll be all right?"

"I have Max, the author," Hope answered with a smile.

Cori chuckled. "He is into it, isn't he? That hat drives me crazy."

"He fancies himself another Sherlock. Maybe he is."

Cori had been gone an hour before the doorbell rang, and when Hope answered, she was surprised to find Pamela Callier standing on the porch.

"Come in," Hope said. "Can I get you something?"

"Wine," the tall woman said. "I need to pick your brain."

"That won't take long," Hope joked.

Pamela pushed up her eyeglasses. "We both know better than that."

"Mind if we drink in the kitchen?"

"I prefer it."

Hope provided the wine and sat opposite Pamela, who spun a gold ring around a finger on her right hand. It was a nervous habit. Hope wondered what made Pamela so nervous.

"How is the investigation going?" Pamela asked.

"I can't speak for the police, but I haven't made much progress."

"Would you tell me if you had?"

Hope shrugged. "I wouldn't have the authorization."

"Exactly. We do the same with relatives of our patients. Unless the patient okays it, we can't tell the relatives much of anything. It drives some people insane, but that's the law. Everyone is entitled to their medical secrets."

"That's not a bad thing."

"No, just darned inconvenient. I want you to know that I had no idea that Boris was a fake. I mean, he had pretty good credentials, and he performed well."

"You were involved in hiring him?" Hope asked.

"I was. There's always a shortage of good nurses. We don't dig too deep into a person's life. That's not good, because killing people in a hospital is not terribly difficult. Don't tell anyone I said that."

"I agree," Hope said. "People die in hospitals. Sometimes, there's no autopsy as the person was sick to begin with. It makes it hard to spot a murder."

"Don't do an Internet search on hospital serial killers. You'll never visit a hospital again." Pamela took a sip from her glass.

"I console myself by remembering that America is one of the safest places in the world."

"True. Back to Boris. Word has it that Gerald found out about Boris and threatened to inform immigration. Is that true?"

Hope nodded. "I believe it probably is."

J. A. WHITING & NELL MCCARTHY

"So, that's the motive. Boris doesn't want to go back to Poland or wherever he came from."

"I can't say I blame him. Although, when you think about it, killing Gerald wouldn't make much sense. I mean, everyone connected to the practice would come under scrutiny. That would include Boris. It wouldn't take the police long to discover his secret."

"What do you think about blackmail?"

"Blackmail?" Hope asked.

"What if Boris was being blackmailed by Gerald. Boris couldn't afford that, and he couldn't run away, as Gerald would make sure the identity theft was well known everywhere. The only way out was to get rid of Gerald."

"If he stole one identity, I think he would be able to steal a second," Hope suggested. "Better to be arrested for theft than murder."

Pamela sipped more wine. "You make a good point. Maybe he was seeing someone and couldn't leave."

"Was he seeing someone with money? I think if he thought he was going to marry into millions, he might stay even after being discovered."

"I wouldn't know."

"Who would?" Hope asked.

"Allison Crush, our psychologist. She and Boris were friends. I think he might have confided in her. And, if she was his doctor, then they would enjoy a special relationship. She couldn't tell anyone about him, I think."

"Confidentiality is honored in most cases, but there are exceptions. Allison might not be able to reveal what he tells her, but that stops at murder. I think she might be obligated to reveal his fake credentials also, in order to protect the other patients."

"I agree. Since he's been arrested, however, Allison might be allowed to tell what she knows."

Hope tapped her glass. "I think I'll have to talk to her. I'm not the police, though. She doesn't have to tell me anything."

"If she's as smart as she thinks she is, she'll tell you everything she knows."

"We'll see."

"You don't like Gerald's brother as a murderer?" Pamela asked.

Hope wagged her head back and forth. "I don't really see it. I mean there's motive, but I'm not sure Harold has the wherewithal to pull off a murder like this."

"And Gerry's wife? I don't know Darlene well, but I think she could do it."

"I agree. The question becomes whether or not Gerald was getting ready to change his will and his insurance policies cutting out Darlene. She would have to act before the changes were made."

"Exactly," Pamela said. "Then, there's me. If I were skimming money and Gerry found out, then I would have to send him to his grave, right?"

"Money is the life blood of murder. People kill for other reasons, but money seems to be the best reason."

"I'll tell you this right now, Hope. When this is over, I'm giving up my managing partner gig. I've had enough."

Hope smiled.

After Pamela left, Max appeared while Hope was rinsing the glasses.

"She really wanted information, didn't she?" Max observed.

"She's scared. I don't blame her. She's afraid she'll get tagged as a murderer. Even if she's never convicted, that sort of thing leaves a tarnish. People won't look at her the same."

"How very true. I suppose that's a vote for her innocence."

"Not necessarily. If she were a very clever killer, she might well try to make us believe that she's trying to save herself. Or, she might be evaluating how close we are to arresting her. In that case, she might bug out tonight and fly to a country that doesn't have an extradition treaty with us."

Max shook his head. "That would be more devious than I am willing to imagine. I would never wish to play you in chess, Mrs. Herring. You would be many steps ahead of me."

"Don't be so sure, Max. I've come to the realization that I can't read minds. To be safe, I have to consider many possible reasons for what someone does."

"You are a master at it. By the way, I hate to admit that I have not been following the feedback from Cori's audition. I'm afraid my writing skills do not include speed. Have you received any word?"

"Not yet. The casting director told us she would call by today. That hasn't happened, so it would seem that Cori didn't get the part."

"The casting director should have called anyway. It's rude not to live up to one's promises."

"It's called ghosting. When someone doesn't answer your email, your texts, calls, or whatever, it's as if he or she has become a ghost. Not a ghost like you, Max. It's just an expression."

"I understand. It's an appropriate term. There are many ghosts out there that never make their presence known. They merely observe. I don't subscribe to that behavior. My interactions with you have been most pleasant and elucidating. I'm glad we have managed as well as we have."

Hope smiled. "No one is more pleased than I am. I'm going to nominate you for ghost of the year."

Max laughed. "That would be most kind, if there were such an award. I like to think we have made a good team."

"The best. It's time for bed. Cori is staying the night with Lottie, as you no doubt know. I've had enough wine for one evening. Are you going to stay up writing?"

"No, I don't think so. I have written my way into a corner. I don't know what's going to happen next."

"Writer's block?"

Max said, "More like writer's remorse. I can't very well make the killer stupid at this point, can I?"

"No, that would cheat the audience. You can have the detective do something dumb. That would be okay to do."

"Villains can't make mistakes?"

"Of course, they can and they do. What they can't do is hand the solution over to the detective on a platter. Sometimes, what the villain does isn't really stupid. It only appears that way."

"How so?" Max questioned.

"I saw a movie once where a suspect went into the victim's bedroom and shot the victim five times."

"He killed like that?"

"He confessed, giving up the weapon and everything, but he couldn't be convicted because the victim was already dead. You can't murder a corpse. You can be charged with some other crimes about mutilating a body, but not murder."

"So, he walked?"

Hope shook her head. "No, he was the real killer. He knifed the victim two hours before he fired the shots. By confessing, he hoped to trick the police. After all, who goes back to the scene of the crime and kills a second time?"

"Very clever. I shall have to remember these tidbits of great detective stories. Perhaps, I can have my villain do something seemingly stupid, only to find out that it was some brilliant ploy that only the hero can see through."

"It's worked in the past." Hope waved and turned out the light.

In bed, she glanced at her phone in the hope there was a message. She knew that Cori would be stewing about the role. They both needed an answer. It seemed the decision was ... silence.

Hope turned off the light and closed her eyes.

Her phone chimed.

She looked at the Caller ID.

Casting Director.

15

"She called from California. I forgot about the time difference."

Hope placed the last cake in the oven and turned to Edsel. The older woman had her brawny arms crossed. Edsel, the owner of the Butter Up Bakery, had taken a liking to both Hope and Cori.

"How big a difference?" Edsel asked.

"Three hours," Hope said. "I thought it was all over because it was bedtime here. There, it was simply the end of a long Friday afternoon."

"So, Cori got the job?"

"For the moment. The details have to be worked out and that's the manager's task. Once that's done, they'll arrange for a screen test."

"They want her to act?" Edsel asked.

"Exactly. While singing is the big deal, Cori needs to do a bit of acting. If that goes well, then they start recording episodes."

"Wow, that's amazing. When can we see them?"

"I'm not sure about the roll out of the series. There's a tentative schedule, but things change. We'll see. I'll let you know."

"You keep an eye on her, Hope. There are all sorts of stories about young girls going wrong when they're in the spotlight."

"I know, and trust me, I'm just as scared as you are. I hope Cori doesn't get her head turned by someone with a glib tongue."

"You raised her right. I think you can trust her. It's the drugs that make things bad."

"We're all capable of mistakes, aren't we?"

"Amen, Hope, amen to that."

Cori was waiting when her mother came home and if Hope hadn't been carrying a celebration cake, the teen would have jumped into her arms. Instead, she simply hugged her from the side.

"Mom, Mom, it's really come true! I can't stop thinking about it."

"I know, Cori, I know. It feels so good, doesn't it?"

"I can't believe it. I'm going to be in a Disney

production. I'm going to sing. I ... please tell me this is real and not some awful joke."

"No joke. You cleared the first hurdle. The next one will be more difficult, and the one after that even higher. It's like running a race up a mountain. Evcry time you think you've reached some sort of pinnacle, you realize that the next peak is higher and steeper. Worse, there's not much time to rest. You have to do the same thing tomorrow and tomorrow and tomorrow."

"It will become a job, won't it?"

"Yep, and like all jobs, there will be times when you don't want to do it. So, the best thing you can do is treat it like a job. You set your alarm, you get out of bed, you make your bed, you dress, you eat break-fast, and you go to work. Of course, getting up in the morning is generally the result of going to bed at a decent time the night before. It becomes easier, if it becomes a habit. You don't do it once in a while. You do it every day."

"Like brushing my teeth?"

"Exactly. Good habits lead to good results."

"In that case, I'll keep brushing."

"Want a piece of cake now or later?"

"Later. I want to invite Lottie over for dinner, is that okay?"

"Sure, ask Adele too. We'll have a big cele-bration."

"Perfect."

With a kiss, Cori ran out of the house leaving Hope to wonder what to cook. No, there would be no cooking. They would have pizza, with wine for her and Adele. If ever there was a time for having some fun, it was this day. While Cori said she was prepared to work for the long haul, Hope knew it wasn't that simple, but she knew Cori could do it. Hope put the cake in the fridge just as the doorbell rang.

Allison Crush smiled. "Sorry I didn't call first, but have you got a few minutes?"

"Sure," Hope said. "Come in. Can I get you something?"

"I'd love a cup of coffee," Allison said.

"This way." Hope led the way to the kitchen.

Allison settled herself at the table while Hope made the coffee. Allison was dressed in weekend garb—jeans, tee, and sandals. It was obvious she wasn't working that day.

"I've been thinking about Boris," Allison said. "This is just speculation, but I think he might have had a thing going with Pamela."

"Pamela?" Hope's face showed surprise. "What kind of thing?"

"You know Pamela was the partner who controlled the money. She also authorized overtime. I think he chatted her up to get the extra hours."

"Do you think Pamela was getting a kickback?" Hope asked.

"Interesting question. I don't know. I will say that I think Boris was charging for more hours than he actually worked."

"That's pretty serious cheating." Hope leaned back in her chair.

"It is, and I would think Pamela would know what he was doing. You know, I always think the best of people, so I never thought Pamela would get into a kickback scheme with Boris, but..."

"Is there some reason Pamela needs more money?"

Allison said, "I don't know much about her circumstances, but I do know her parents are pretty sick. Medical conditions can drain a bank account quickly."

"Tell me about it. Without insurance a lot of people would be filing for bankruptcy. So, Pamela paid Boris for hours he didn't work, and then he split the money with her?"

Allison shrugged. "That's a guess. I have no idea how long it's been going on. It would be worth many thousands if they were at it for a while."

"Until Gerald discovered the scam?"

"Could be." Allison wrapped her hands around her coffee mug. "We could be barking up the wrong tree." She smiled. "Here, I came to see what you think, and I'm the one who's speculating on what might have happened."

"It's nothing that I haven't wondered about. Do you think he and she are involved romantically?" Hope asked.

"I don't see how," Allison said. "Boris is something of a lowbrow, if you know what I mean. Pamela is a class or two above him. They could work together, but I don't see them as a couple. She's champagne and he's light beer."

"I think you're right about that." Hope nodded.

"We know that Gerry died of a fentanyl overdose. Do you think that's a Pamela thing, or would Boris opt for that?"

Hope said, "Poison is generally a female method, but I wouldn't put it past Boris. He would certainly be well aware of what fentanyl can do."

"You know, I think I have a bead on Pamela. She's clever. She probably knows that an overdose would point to her. I'm going to tag Boris with the murder, since poison is not preferred by males," Allison said.

"He's smart enough for that?"

"It doesn't take a genius," Allison told her.

"Exactly."

"Enough of that," Allison said. "I heard your daughter is a singer? I also heard she's trying out for some big part in a Hollywood movie?"

Hope beamed. "She's a very good singer. She landed a part, temporarily, in a Disney production. I don't know everything, but if it works out, she'll be filming at Disney studios."

"Congratulations! That's terrific. Gosh, I wish I could sing. I'm tone deaf. I mean it, really tone deaf. I can't carry a tune in a bucket."

After Allison left, Hope made her way to the attic. She found Max pacing the office, deerstalker hat and unlit pipe in place.

"Did you know, Mrs. Herring, that Sherlock Holmes liked to pace his flat while considering the facts of a case."

"He also took opium, didn't he?"

"Yes, his drug habits are well known. In those days, before modern painkillers, laudanum was popular. Given that people often suffered from tooth decay and debilitating pain, using drugs was not totally frowned upon. Laudanum was espe-cially good for females who didn't wish to drink spirits."

Hope said, "I'm not sure we've advanced very far from those days. People still seek all manner of ways to reduce pain. A lot of drug use is fueled by emotional pain. People don't think they should ever feel bad."

"That does seem to be the mantra of the times. No need to grieve or be depressed or feel unloved. Just pop a pill and make your troubles disappear."

"Unfortunately, those pain pills can sometimes kill you."

Max stopped and doffed his hat to her. "You must excuse me. I need to congratulate you again on Cori's success. I also must ask you a question. Since she will be in some other state, I think?"

Hope nodded.

"You aren't thinking of moving, are you?"

Hope shook her head. "Not in the short term, Max. Cori's success is not guaranteed. I am a teacher who has a contract till the end of the school year. I am not going to quit now."

"Quite right. I just wanted you to know that if you decide to move, that is perfectly all right with me. I will take that as a sign from the universe that I should move along also. I see no reason to stay if you and Cori are not here."

"Max, I...you don't have to do that. You certainly don't need to move just because we do."

"I have succeeded beyond my wildest dreams, Mrs. Herring. You and Cori have opened up the world for me. That said, I know when it's time to bid adieu. Not now, not yet. When you're gone. I do not wish to stay here all alone. Sounds sentimental, doesn't it? I went a century without human interaction. I do not wish to repeat that. I believe I can find some companionship with the spirits that have gone before me, and I would like to see my family again. I intend to find out."

Hope felt a pang of sorrow in her heart. Like Max, she had come to rely on their friendship.

"I never meant to find friendship with a ghost," Hope said, "but I'm very glad I did."

Max bowed.

With a smile, Hope nodded.

Adele and Lottie arrived at dusk and Hope handed Adele a glass of wine.

"When are you moving?" Adele asked.

"I'm not moving," Hope answered. "A single audition is not a reason to put the house on the market. I think you know that."

"I know, I know. If you do want to sell, will you tell me first? I have a friend who would like to move here, provided I can come up with a suitable house. Yours would be perfect."

"You're on. You'll be the first to know."

The pizza arrived and everyone started eating. The table talk was quick and funny. The mood was just what Hope had hoped for. When her phone chimed, she thought about not answering, but her conscience got the better of her.

"Hello, Pamela," Hope said.

"Hope, you have to come now."

"I'm sorry. I'm in the middle of a celebration. Cori got a singing gig."

Pamela said, "Great for her. I'm in Boris's house. He's dead."

16

Hope used a tissue to push open the door to the house Boris rented. The porch was dark, with no outside lights. She called out as she stepped inside.

"Pamela?!"

"In here."

Light spilled out of the dining room where Hope found Pamela sitting on the floor.

"Where is he?" Hope asked.

Pamela pointed to the far end of the table. Szymon sat in a chair, his chest a bloody mess.

"He's dead?" Hope asked.

"Very," Pamela answered.

Hope noticed a revolver on the table. She approached but didn't touch it.

"I found it there," Pamela said. "Right before I grabbed it."

"You touched it?" Hope tilted her head to the side.

"I heard someone in the kitchen. I wasn't really thinking. I thought I might need a weapon, so I picked it up."

Hope asked, "Was there someone in the kitchen?"

"No, but the back door was open. I closed it."

"You didn't see anyone?"

"No, no one."

"You know how this looks, don't you?" Hope questioned.

Pamela nodded and held out her hand. "I do. My prints will be on the gun. I don't know if the police will find any other prints or anything in the kitchen. If they don't, then I'm the main suspect. I'd think the same thing."

"Did you call the police?" Hope pulled Pamela to her feet.

"No, I wanted to talk to you first and because Boris was already dead. No one could help him."

"I called Detective Robinson before I left the house. He'll be here soon. You didn't hear the gunshots?"

"No, I didn't."

"All right," Hope said as she looked about the room. "Tell me what you're doing here."

"Boris called me. He said we needed to talk. I didn't want to come, but he said it was important, something about Gerald's death so I got in my car and came over. I found him like this."

"Let's go to the other room," Hope suggested. "That's when you heard someone in the kitchen?"

"Yes, and I grabbed the gun."

"That you put back."

"I ... I didn't know what to do. I put it back and thought I could just leave. You know, let someone else find the body."

"Why didn't you?"

"For one thing, I had already touched the back door and the front door and who knows what else in this place. I couldn't wipe away the fingerprints."

"You didn't wipe the gun?"

"No. I ... I didn't think to. I panicked. The first thing I could think to do was call you."

They stood in the middle of the big living room. Nothing seemed out of place. To Hope's eye, there had not been any kind of struggle.

"That isn't your firearm?" Hope asked.

Pamela shook her head. "I own one. After

dealing with Rowdy Sherman, I bought a Sig, as the gunsmith called it. A good gun. I can shoot it." The woman took a deep breath. "I'm in big trouble, aren't I?"

"I won't lie to you. I think you're telling the truth, but you could be lying. The evidence is decidedly against you. Did you have a motive? Do you stand to gain from his death?"

"No, I don't get a thing out of this. You have to believe that."

"Was he blackmailing you?"

"For what?"

"The murder of Gerald Pantini."

"No. No." Tears welled in Pamela's eyes. "I had nothing to do with that."

Hope thought a second. A siren could be heard in the distance. "The police are coming. I recommend you tell them what you told me."

"I shouldn't get a lawyer?"

"That's up to you."

"The evidence is all against me."

"It appears that way."

"Crap, Hope, I don't stand a chance."

"You never know what they might uncover. They might find evidence of another person in the house. Someone might have heard the gunshots before you arrived. A neighbor walking the dog could have seen the other person."

"Lots of speculation there."

"Do what you have to do."

The cruiser, lights flashing, stopped in front of the house. Hope used her tissue to open the door for the patrolman.

"I called Detective Robinson," she said.

"He's on his way."

Hope waited outside in her car while the police processed the scene. It was murder through and through. That would dictate much of their response. When she saw the detective approaching, she slipped out of her SUV.

"How is she?" Hope asked.

"Silent," he answered. "She lawyered up."

"I'm sorry about that."

"Me too. I take it she talked to you?"

Hope nodded. "I can tell you what she said, and I suppose I can testify in court, if it comes to that."

"You can. So, fill me in. I think when she realizes she's already confessed, she'll talk to me too."

"She didn't confess. In fact, she said she found the victim exactly as you found him."

"You believe her?"

"I do, and I don't. She also said she picked up the

gun and closed the kitchen door. You'll find her prints."

"We bagged her hands. We'll do a GSR test at the station. So, she admitted handling the murder weapon?"

"She did. She said there was someone in the kitchen, and she was afraid. Not thinking, she grabbed the gun for protection."

"Believe her?"

Hope shrugged. "She's a trained physician. She's been under pressure before. How many times did she panic?"

"So, you don't buy her story."

"I'm not sure. That she asked for an attorney tells me she isn't thinking clearly, as I would be forced to testify against her. Well, not for her."

"Start at the beginning."

"It started with a celebration pizza party. Cori landed a role in a Disney production."

"She did? Congratulations! That's terrific. That would be cause for some joy."

"Yes, well, that's when I got the call from Pamela. She was here. She had found the body, although she didn't say that. She just said the man was dead."

Hope walked Robinson through the next half

hour, as she drove to the house and found Pamela on the floor next to the dead man.

"On the floor?"

"She didn't want to leave more prints."

"But she already handled the murder weapon."

"Like I said, I'm not sure she was thinking right."

"Or, she was thinking very well. She was setting up her defense."

"She could have wiped off the gun and walked out. No one knew she was here. I don't think anyone knew."

"There's the phone call from Szymon," Derrick said. "Her car was here. People might have noticed."

"True, but she's still better off cleaning the gun and leaving. You find her prints in the house, and she says she and Szymon were colleagues. Of course, she's been to his house in the past."

"Motive. Why would she kill him?"

"Pantini. You're aware that he discovered some money missing from the partnership. Szymon knew Pamela was stealing and was blackmailing her. She decided to end it."

"That sounds plausible. After all, if she offed Pantini, would she hesitate with Szymon?"

Hope shrugged. "She said someone else stole the money and set her up. Could that happen twice? Is she clever enough to plan two murders where she seems like the best suspect?"

"You know me. I go where the evidence leads, and right now, the evidence points to Pamela Callier."

By the time Hope reached her house, the party was over. Lottie and Adele had left and Cori was asleep. Max met Hope in the kitchen, which had been cleaned.

"I take it someone died," Max said.

"Murdered," she answered. "Szymon Mazur. Shot three times in the chest. Pamela Callier was sitting on the floor when I arrived. She said she didn't do it, but her prints will be found on the murder weapon and around the house. She claims she had no reason to kill him, but there may have been one, if she was stealing from the partnership."

"Do you think she's innocent, Mrs. Herring?"

"I do, and I don't. There was no sign that someone else was inside the house. Her excuse for touching the gun was flimsy. In court, I don't think she stands a chance."

"I see. Someone set her up?"

"That would be her argument. I don't see it. I don't see a reason to do it. Before his death, I was thinking it was Szymon who was stealing the money.

He killed Pantini when Pantini found out about it. After all, Szymon was an admitted criminal. He's here illegally, and he stole someone's identity. I wasn't inclined to believe him."

"People lie, don't they? I must remember that when I'm writing. It makes for a better mystery if people lie and hold back the truth."

"That works in books and movies because it works in real life. Everyone lies to some extent, even if it's just to oneself."

"I will let you get to bed. Good night, Mrs. Herring."

"Good night, Max."

Hope was grading essays at her desk when Detective Robinson walked into the classroom. The students were gone for the day and with no lesson with Norrie scheduled, Cori had ridden home with Lottie. Hope was glad that the two were spending time together. Cori would soon be on a sound stage for good or ill. Hope prayed that she was not making a mistake.

"Did everyone get all A's?" the detective asked.

"Hardly," she answered. "It seems that every year

the writing gets worse. Not for all my students but for enough. They don't bother to look up correct spelling or complete sentences. Putting together a persuasive paragraph is beyond their ability. I'm not encouraged."

"The cost of trying to boost egos, I suppose," he said. "My own children think close is good enough."

"Perhaps, it is. I don't know. I have students that think they're Shakespeare. In reality, their work is closer to bad song lyrics. We could go on for a day about the lack of precision, but that's not why you're here."

Derrick said, "I just wanted to check a couple of things you told me."

"Pamela's still not talking?"

He shook his head. "Her lawyer told her to remain mum. It doesn't matter really. The case is getting stronger by the hour."

"How so?" Hope asked.

"Pamela told you that she was there because Szymon called her, correct?"

"That's what she said."

"We checked his phone. He never called her, not last night."

Hope shook her head. "Why would she lie about something so easily checked?"

"She needed a reason to be there."

"You checked her phone?"

"Yes, she allowed that," Derrick explained. "She did receive a call around the time she said, but it was from a burner phone. There's no way to know who called."

"You checked the nearest cell tower to the murder scene?"

"Doing that now. I can tell you for certain that we did not find a burner inside the house."

"So, Szymon never made the call?"

"It's looking that way. If we find the burner in Pamela's house, well, we can surmise that she called herself to establish her alibi."

"The murder weapon?" Hope asked.

"Still tracing it. I wouldn't be surprised if it was reported stolen at some point."

"Doesn't sound like the plan of an intelligent person, does it?"

"Oh, I don't know," Derrick considered. "There might be enough there for some capable attorney to instill reasonable doubt in a jury. No witnesses, no confirmed motive. It might have happened like she said."

"You don't believe that."

"Nope. Neither do you. I think she's been playing

you and me all along. She stole the money and got caught, so she killed Pantini. When Szymon figured it out, she decided he had to go too. In both instances, she points to herself as the prime suspect and denies she had anything to do with the deaths."

Hope suggested, "If you're going to get blamed, create as much confusion as possible?"

"Looks like it. I mean, we will find other fingerprints in Szymon's house. We did come up with a handful of suspects for the Pantini murder. Muddy the water enough and the jury can't see the fish."

Detective Robinson waved as he left. Hope thought a minute before she returned to the essays. They hadn't become any better, which made her sigh.

When she pulled into her drive, she spotted Rowdy Sherman sitting on the steps leading to the porch. She climbed out of her vehicle as he approached.

"Can I help you?" she asked.

"Did you know there's a man inside your house?"

17

"What?" For a moment, Hope couldn't quite process what Rowdy had said.

"When no one answered my knock, I walked around the house thinking you might be in back. I peeked into the kitchen, and there was a guy in a weird hat sitting at the table."

"Are you certain?"

"I know what I saw."

"I'm afraid you're mistaken. I'm sure there's no one inside."

"Don't try to tell me what I saw. My shrink does that and it really ticks me off. Got that?"

Hope stepped back. "Certainly. All right, let's go inside and we'll see if anyone is there."

"He didn't look like a regular guy so I'll do the heavy lifting, if it comes to that."

"I'm sure that won't be necessary."

Hope unlocked the door and led the way. She was sure that Max had disappeared long before they entered.

"Follow me," Hope said.

The kitchen was empty except for the cat heading toward Hope. "Maybe he spotted you and went out the door." Even as she spoke, she saw the lock on the back door turn. "Try the door."

Rowdy went to the door and pulled it open. "You're right. It's unlocked. You might look about to see if he took something."

Hope did a quick scan knowing that nothing was missing. "Nope, all seems in place. I have to thank you for that, Mr. Sherman."

"Glad to help. You should be more careful about locking your doors."

"I'm sure I'll be very careful in the future. Now, what can I help you with?"

"I hear there's been another murder," Rowdy said.

"I'm afraid so. A man named Boris Green was shot and killed in his own home."

"I heard that. I know Boris. He worked with that medical group that killed off my son."

"Did he have anything to do with your son?"

"No, I got no quarrel with Boris," Rowdy told her. "He was all right. I just heard about him, and I thought I should tell you something. I can't tell the police because they don't do squat, even when they got reason to do something. I don't know if it means anything, but I was out and about the other day. I happened by where he was living. It was getting dark, so I couldn't make out everything. But he was having words with a woman on the front porch."

Hope narrowed her eyes. "You're sure it was Boris?"

"Yes, ma'am. He was wearing that ankle gizmo that the police give you to keep you from going anywhere. I know. I had one of them things once. They're electronic chains."

"Who was the woman?"

"I couldn't see. She was in the shadows."

"Her voice?"

"She wasn't yellin' like Boris was," Rowdy explained.

"Could it have been Dr. Pamela Callier?" Hope asked.

Rowdy shrugged. "Maybe. Like I said, I wasn't that close."

"But you're sure they were arguing?"

Rowdy bristled. "Don't be telling me what I know and what I don't know. I don't know any more than that. The two of them were going at it."

"All right, but why come to me? Why not go to the police?"

"I got no trust in the police. When I needed them, they turned their back on me. I wouldn't help them for nothin.'"

"I understand and I appreciate the information. I will have to pass it along to the police. Do you remember what time it was?"

"Well, it was gettin' dark, so say close to seven-thirty maybe," Rowdy said.

"Great, good, thanks."

"I'm doin' this cause Boris was nice to me. He didn't think I was some kind of whacko."

"I'm sure he would appreciate your effort," Hope told the man.

Rowdy turned away and then turned back. "You don't think I'm a whack job, do you?"

"No, I don't. I think you were a father who wanted what was best for his son and couldn't get it."

"That's right. You got me, ma'am, you got me."

Rowdy was long gone before Max appeared in the kitchen.

"Mrs. Herring, I must apologize," he said sheepishly.

"It was bound to happen, Max. People are nosey. I imagine more than one person has spotted you inside the house, but simply didn't have the courage to tell me about it. They probably thought I had a man in my life. Most of them might even be happy about that."

"You do have a man in your life. Luke is a very nice man. You're far too young and comely to live without companionship."

Hope had been seeing Luke casually for a while. He owned a landscaping company and was often away on business. She enjoyed his company, but they were taking it slow. She thought he was a good man, kind, caring, supportive and was happy he was in her life.

"I haven't given up. I have a daughter to raise, and it appears that particular task will become even more difficult. However, I do have a man around. I have Luke. And I have you, Max. You are worth far more than most of the other men in this town."

"Thank you for saying that, but I'm afraid I let you down. I shall do better, Mrs. Herring. I promise. I have taken my status for granted. That won't happen again."

When Max disappeared, Hope smiled. She could admit to herself that Max was one of the best men she had ever met—outside of her deceased husband, and Luke.

Max was ... extraordinary.

Hope sat by herself in the interrogation room. The two coffees in front of her were growing cold. What was keeping Robinson? She needed to get home to Cori. She needed to finish some school tasks. Hope didn't have all night. The door opened. Detective Robinson escorted Pamela into the room. She was cuffed, and Robinson shackled her cuffs to the table.

"Is that necessary?" Hope whispered.

"Department rules," Robinson said. "For everyone's protection."

"I don't mind," Pamela said, "not too much."

"This won't take long, Pamela, I promise," the detective said.

"Take all the time you want. My cell isn't exactly a five-star hotel."

"I think we're all sorry about that," Hope told her.

"I didn't kill anyone, Hope. You have to believe that."

"I want to, I do, but like Detective Robinson, I have to follow the facts."

"The fact is I didn't shoot Boris."

"What did you and Boris argue about?" the detective asked.

"Everything. Well, not everything. He was always cutting corners and then trying to get overtime for screwing up. I don't like approving overtime when it isn't needed."

"What did you argue about the night he died?"

"We didn't argue about anything." Pamela looked down at the table. "He was dead when I got there."

"Before he died, he was seen arguing with a woman on the porch of his house."

"Was I identified?"

"No, just a woman who could have been you."

"It wasn't me."

"This is not a time to lie," Detective Robinson warned.

"I'm not lying. You can check my car GPS. I was in Wilmington all day. I drove straight from there to Boris's house. It wasn't me on that porch with him."

"We will check, so lying won't help."

"Let me repeat. I am not lying. I wasn't the woman on the porch."

Hope stood. "Thank you, Pamela. I needed to clear that up."

"Time to go back," Robinson said.

"Can you give me another minute to sip coffee? The cell is ... dismal."

"Take a minute. I need to talk with Detective Robinson."

Hope led the detective out of the interrogation room and they stopped in the corridor.

"I believe her," Hope said. "The GPS data is too easy to check."

"I know, but it doesn't matter. If she wasn't arguing with Szymon, that's fine. Her prints are still on the murder weapon. Her hands still tested positive for GSR. When she reached the house doesn't really matter."

"No, but it might tell us there's another suspect. If Szymon and someone were arguing vehemently, then that woman might have murdered him and framed Pamela with the call."

Derrick ran his hand through his hair. "Possibly, but that's a real stretch."

"You have to investigate that because it will come

up in the courtroom. You don't want to tell a jury that you simply ignored the information."

"You make a good point. All right, we'll canvass the area and see if any neighbors witnessed the argument. That won't stop the prosecution of Callier."

"I know that. It will, however, remove doubt as to her guilt. That's important."

Hope returned to the house to find Cori and Max chatting in the kitchen. They were both grinning ear to ear.

"Mom, Max did some searching on the net and discovered the website for the new show I'm in."

"Remember, you have to sign a contract first."

"I can do that easy. I'm so excited."

"It's a wonderful opportunity. We're all excited for you." Hope hugged her daughter.

"I'm need to finish my homework and go practice, but I can barely think straight I'm so happy."

"Just do what you can," Hope suggested.

"I will." Cori left the room.

Hope turned to Max. "She's gung-ho about this, isn't she?"

"As she should be," Max said. "It's new, and it's daydream material. If I were her, I'd be accepting my Oscar about now."

Hope laughed at the ghost's comment, but then turned serious. "It all makes me so nervous. Cori's so young. I hope we're doing the right thing."

"Cori has a good head on her shoulders. She's sensible, she works hard, she's not afraid to go after what she wants. If this doesn't work out, she'll pour herself into the next thing she's interested in. She will do just fine, Mrs. Herring."

"I read something once about a screenwriter who sold a screenplay and then stopped, waiting for the movie to be made. When that happened, he thought a lot of doors would open. That is exactly the wrong thing to do. He should have started on that next script, that next contact, that next idea. No matter what happened to that first script, waiting was a horrible strategy. If he sold one, he could sell another. He needed the 'never wait' attitude."

"Good artists are like that, aren't they? They paint a picture, put it up for sale, and immediately start the next picture. They can't have a showing, if there's only one good picture. Cori will never sit around waiting for something to happen. She's a doer. She's resilient."

"It's like being an author. As soon as you finish book one, you have to start book two. You can't wait till book one is published."

"Agreed. I should probably be working out the plot now, right? Outlining? Building characters? Finding a suitable location? It's a good lesson to learn, Mrs. Herring. I must never wait. I have to keep moving forward."

Hope thought that Max had waited around too long already. Perhaps, he should not have waited around in order to solve his own murder. She was not going to point that out because she didn't want him to leave.

"Speaking of never waiting," Hope said, "I have some schoolwork to finish." She smiled at the ghost. "You'll secure the perimeter?"

"Absolutely. No one will get in while I am here. I must exercise my own good habits."

When Max disappeared, Hope traipsed up the steps to her attic office. As she settled behind the computer, she couldn't help but wonder about the woman Szymon argued with. It could have been anyone, but who was the most likely? How could Hope find out? Was the woman involved with Pantini? Was it Pantini's estranged wife? That might make sense, if Szymon had provided the fentanyl capsules that killed Gerald. Certainly, Szymon would know how to acquire the drug.

Hope shook her head. She was letting her brain

wander off into the swamp when she needed to concentrate. She had a job to do. She couldn't display the procrastination she preached against.

Never wait.

She had forgotten about that lesson. She needed to focus on her real job, and then she'd come up with a way to chat with Darlene Pantini.

18

—————

"I can't do it."

"What can't you do?" Hope asked.

"I can't do the Disney thing," Cori said.

Hope wanted to tell Cori that driving to school was not the time or place for this discussion. Instead, she asked the obvious question.

"Why not?"

"I'm not ready. It's all happened so fast, and I'm not ready. I'll flub it up and lose my chance."

"Everyone makes mistakes. Everyone fails. If you fail, you fail. One failure means very little in the greater scheme of your life."

"What if they dump me? What if they tell everyone that I couldn't cut it?"

"This is nothing more than what is called cold

feet. You're scared of failing, and you might be scared of success. Part of you might think that you're not worthy of this opportunity. So, like lots of people, you sabotage yourself. Sometimes, I think half the miserable people in the world are people who are scared of becoming successful. Those people, at crucial moments, come in unprepared or drunk or don't show up at all, and then the opportunity they had evaporates. They become what they secretly thought they were ... failures."

"Like the kids who don't study for a test?"

"Exactly. For some reason, they skip doing the work and then wonder why they're not a huge success. Don't be your own worst enemy. Prepare for your role. Do the best you can. If it doesn't work out, it will be okay. Failure just points out the need to improve or the need to do something in a different way."

"Yeah, that makes sense. I'm just scared, I guess."

"Make it a fun thing. Accept the challenge and see where it takes you. If it doesn't work out, you had an experience most others never will. Most people never find out just how good they can be. They stop short because they're afraid."

"That's what Norrie says. If you never reach for that high note, you'll never discover your range."

"Take it from Norrie. Do your best. By the way, I believe your manager has worked out the details of your contract. Pretty standard by all accounts. Now, it's just a matter of being Cori Herring."

"Think I should change my name?"

"Change it? Why?"

"I read where a lot of famous actors change their names to something that's easily remembered."

"I don't think you have to think about that yet. In today's world, a lot of actors don't change their names."

"Just wondering."

"Talk to your manager. She might recommend something."

"Good idea."

Hope pushed Cori's issues to the side and focused on her students. Halloween was only three weeks away, and it was a major event in the lives of children. Vampires, ghosts, black cats, and witches captured the imagination of the young. Imagination, fun, and being someone else for a night.

During her lunch break, Hope called Darlene Pantini. Since Darlene didn't pick up, she left a voicemail. They needed to talk about Boris. During the afternoon, Hope checked her phone several times, but Darlene didn't call back. Hope wondered if she needed to talk to Detective Robinson. He might be able to get Darlene's attention. She was on her way to Norrie's with Cori in the backseat, when the call came.

"Hello, Darlene," Hope said. "When can we meet?"

The address was in a section of Castle Park that Hope had not visited before. As she pulled to the curb, she noticed some activity in the garage, whose door was up. Several women were engaged in some activity Hope didn't recognize until she approached. They were making posters and signs. Spray paint cans sat atop a card table. The large signs leaned against a wall.

NO OIL

SAVE THE WHALES

THE PLANET IS BURNING

Hope recognized the making of a protest. Something was going to happen soon.

Darlene stepped out of the garage. She grinned, happy to be doing what she was doing. Hope recognized the signs of drinking. On another table were several bottles of wine and red plastic cups. The women might as well be giddy in their work.

"What's with the signs?" Hope asked.

"Big protest in Raleigh. Our stupid representatives want to allow offshore drilling. Here we're facing the hottest year ever, and they want to burn off more oil and gas. Make sense? Heck no. We're going to show our strength. The last thing we need is drilling on the Outer Banks."

Hope changed the subject. "How well did you know Boris Green?"

"Not all that well, but I will confess to a one-night stand. I was in a bar, and he walked in. We had a few drinks. We both had the itch. It was a terrible idea, but then, I'm full of terrible ideas. I was gone before he woke up in the morning."

"It was just that one time?"

"Yep. He thought he was some kind of great lover. Nope. Pretty ordinary."

"When did you see him last?"

"Hmm, that was ages ago. Well, not really ages, but months anyway. Why?"

"You weren't at his house the night he died?"

Darlene shook her head. "I don't think I could find his house. I was there exactly once and I didn't work at keeping that memory alive."

"The night he died Boris had a heated argument with a woman. I'm trying to find out who it was."

"Good luck with that. I don't know many women

who would admit to an argument with a man who was murdered."

"I agree. Well, thanks for your time."

"No prob. Hey, we can always use more protesters, if you're in the mood. I can drive."

"Thanks, but I have my own demons to face."

Darlene laughed. "Oh, honey, demons never go away."

On the way back to Norrie's house, Hope placed a call to Detective Robinson. Had he had any luck finding the woman that was with Boris the night he died?

"Sorry," the detective said. "No one wants to embrace the encounter. I'm still looking."

"Think Harold Pantini would know?"

"I don't see how. I don't think he and Szymon were pals."

"You never know. I'll check it out."

While Hope waited in her SUV, she phoned Harold, who answered right away.

"Hello," Harold slurred.

"Harold, this is Hope Herring. I have a question for you. How well did you know Boris Green?"

"Who?"

"Green. He was a nurse affiliated with the medical practice your brother kept the books for."

"I … no, I didn't know him at all. Wait, maybe I did see him once or twice. Maybe in Gerry's office. I think… No, no, that doesn't make much sense. I don't think… Listen, my mind is a bit fuzzy."

Hope knew where the fuzziness came from. Harold was mostly drunk. Nothing he remembered would be worth anything.

"It's all right, Harold. I thought you might remember something."

"Not me. You should check with Amber, the shrink."

"You mean Allison?"

"Is that her name? Crap, I … my brain. Check with her."

"I'll do that."

"Hey, hey, wait. You figure out who killed my brother?"

"No, not yet."

"She did it, that doc. She fed him those pills."

"Maybe. Get some rest, Harold."

"Yeah, yeah, I'll do that."

Hope killed the connection and took Harold's advice. She called Allison and left a message. It made sense that the psychologist in the group would know more about the individual members.

Before Cori finished the lesson with Norrie and

came out to the car, Hope received a call from Cori's manager.

"It's done," the manager said. "It needs your signature and Cori's signature. I'll email the documents. Read them carefully, as they're the basis for her employment. If you want, run them past your attorney. That's not necessary as it's a standard contract. However, I want you to be comfortable with what you're signing so do what you have to do. Of course, the sooner you can get the docs back to me, the better. The peeps in California and Florida understand contractual timelines, but they're always pressing for faster work."

"Got it," Hope said. "And thank you. We appreciate it."

"Keep Cori on the straight and narrow. Everything will be fine."

"I'm sure it will."

Cori slid into the SUV, just as Hope put down her phone.

"Your manager called," Hope said. "The contract is finished. It just needs a thorough review and signatures."

"Cool. You're going to sign it, right?"

"You're going to review it, right?" Hope asked.

Cori laughed. "Okay, okay. I'll read it, but I probably won't understand half of it."

Hope chuckled. "Then, read it again. The surest way to keep from being cheated is to understand what you're agreeing to. History is full of people who lost their money because they trusted someone else to read the fine print. If you have questions, ask me or ask your manager. You should always have a good working knowledge of your commitments."

"Roger that." Cori whooped. "I'm going to be in a series. How about that?!"

Hope laughed with her. "It's as fine as frog hair, and that's very fine indeed."

She was in the kitchen fixing salmon with broccolini when her phone chimed.

"Hello, Allison," Hope said.

"You wanted to talk to me?"

"I do. I'm in the middle of fixing dinner. Can we talk later?"

"I'll be busy then. I have a late appointment. That's the trouble with being a psychologist. You have to be available when your patients aren't working. How about tomorrow?"

"Sure, after school. Where shall we meet?"

"Your house? I can be there by four or so. I'll call when I'm on my way."

"Great. No practice for Cori tomorrow so it should work out."

"By the way, what do you want to know?" Allison asked.

"It has to do with Boris Green's murder. I'm looking for some background info on him."

"I thought Pamela killed him. I heard she fired the gun and everything."

"That's the working theory, but the police have to be thorough. If they zero in on one suspect to the exclusion of others, they'll get eaten alive in court."

"I see, yes, that makes sense. Well, I didn't run around with Boris, but I'll give you what I know."

"Great, thanks. See you tomorrow."

The call ended, and Hope turned back to making dinner as Cori entered the room and handed Hope a stack of pages.

"It's the contract," Cori said. "This is your copy. I have my own, and I'm going to my room to read it."

"You can't just give me the highlights?"

"Nope. You have to read it too, Mom. We both need to know and agree on what we know. I'm not going into this without you by my side."

Hope took the pages and laid them on the counter. The contract wasn't overlong, but it was much longer than one page. She wondered whatever happened to the one-page agreement. I do this, you do that. It seemed the more attorneys were involved, the more paragraphs to read. The law was becoming too complicated for the ordinary person.

"The gears of success are meshing?" Max asked.

"Indeed, they are," Hope answered.

Max had exchanged his deerstalker hat for a black beret. With his mustache, he could have passed for a Frenchman.

"Why the beret?" Hope asked.

"Hercule Poirot. I am using my little gray cells like any good Parisian."

"I believe Hercule was from Belgium."

"Well, he was practically French and I'm certain the Belgians wear berets all the time."

"I bet they do. Are those little gray cells firing on all cylinders?" Hope kidded.

"They are, I think. I have come to the conclusion that Agatha Christie was a keen student of humanity. So often, her mysteries center on the emotions of the killers. It isn't always money."

"Humans kill for many reasons. I suppose serial killers are rarely in it for money. It's the thrill, the rush. That probably makes them more dangerous. The usual motives don't apply."

"Well, Agatha dealt with a more genteel society.

Serial killers were not the rage back then. People didn't kill just to kill. At least, it's that way in her books."

"Emotions are powerful things. You can use them to your advantage in your books."

"I intend to, Mrs. Herring, I intend to. If you wish, I would be happy to look over Cori's contract. I am no lawyer, but I did deal with contracts in my day."

"Have at it, Max. I appreciate every set of eyes that wades through the pages."

"My pleasure."

When Max scooped up the pages and walked out of the room, Hope finished making the dinner. She suddenly wondered if Rowdy had lied to her about the argument. What if he was the killer? Wouldn't he feed her a lie to send her down the rabbit hole? She hadn't considered that. Maybe, Allison could shed some light on it.

19

Detective Robinson stopped by the school just before the bell rang for dismissal. He stood at the back of the room and waited for the students to clear. They paid no attention to him, which was fine with Hope. She didn't want to explain his presence to her students. He came forward as the last student exited.

"Got a minute?" he asked.

"Sure," Hope said. "What's on your mind?"

"Szymon Mazur."

"I'm afraid I'm not much help there. Pamela Callier is the most likely killer, but I can't be certain. Something feels off about it."

Derrick nodded. "I know. I'm also guessing he had something to do with the scam that probably got Gerald killed. My question is why didn't he come to us? He might have cleared up some problems."

"Again, I don't know. The usual explanation is blackmail. Maybe he was using his knowledge to bleed Gerald's killer."

"Then that would be Pamela. If Szymon were blackmailing her, then she would have a perfect motive to kill him."

Hope said, "True, but if she worked out the near-perfect murder of Gerald with pills would she then murder someone with a simple shooting? One where she's the prime suspect?"

Derrick looked dejected. "It doesn't make sense, does it? Unless, she had the audacity to lie to our faces over and over."

"She doesn't strike me as being that kind of killer. It takes a pretty cold heart to murder and then deny all the evidence."

"True, but we don't know of anyone who would want to frame her for the murder. Did you have any luck finding the woman who argued with Mazur before he died?"

Hope shook her head. "I'm not sure there was an argument. Rowdy is the only witness to that, and he might have made it all up."

"Pushing the guilt away from himself? Is he that clever?"

"I think so. If you watch a couple of TV crime shows, you could learn how to lie in order to thwart the police."

"They all lie, don't they?" Derrick sighed.

"It seems that way. You can hardly blame them when a vacation in prison is on the table."

"I guess we learn to tell fibs early. How many children admit to raiding the cookie jar?"

"Very few," Hope agreed. "It's easier to blame an invisible friend."

"Indeed."

Hope watched the detective leave. Like him, she was no closer to naming the mystery woman who Rowdy overheard. Was Rowdy lying? Probably, in some fashion. A small lie was sometimes as successful as a big one.

Cori was bubbly, almost giddy on the ride home. She chattered on about Disney and singing and how "cool" it was going to be. Hope didn't interrupt. Cori needed to dream, and this dream was ready to come true.

"Did you ever read the *The Great Gatsby*?" Hope asked.

"Nope. Why? Is it good?"

"It's a classic, an American classic. It's about a man who does everything he can to further his dream. It's been made into a movie more than once."

"It's about dreams?"

"In a way. Gatsby was in love with this woman named Daisy, who was rich while he was poor. In the era before the wars, Gatsby had no chance to marry Daisy, despite their love. That didn't happen in those days. Parents didn't always arrange marriages, but they were pretty good at keeping the riffraff out of the family."

"Sounds horrible."

"It was, and it wasn't. Gatsby went to Europe and served in World War One. He got a medal, I think, and was sent to England. He couldn't get back to the states right away. Since Daisy didn't hear from Gatsby, she ended up marrying another man, a rich man and they started their lives as a privileged couple. Was it a good marriage? Not really, but they managed. Anyway, Gatsby got involved with some rich gangsters. It doesn't matter, because he's not really a gangster himself. The story isn't about that. Gatsby bought a huge house across the water from Daisy. He knows she's there, but she doesn't know he's close. Gatsby threw huge, elaborate parties, hoping that Daisy and Tom would show up. One night, they do. Daisy and Gatsby rekindle the love they felt before the war."

Cori narrowed her eyes. "Is this going someplace I would recognize?"

"Bear with me. While Gatsby wasn't married, Daisy was. That complicated things. Divorce wasn't easy or common in those days. He told Daisy they could make it. She wasn't so sure. Her husband got suspicious and discovered Gatsby's gangster ties. The story boils down to this. Gatsby lived for the dream of being with Daisy. That kept him alive in the war, and it fueled his life after. It was always Daisy, Daisy, Daisy. He had this vision of what would happen when they met. Reality is often cruel. Gatsby's reality didn't match his dream. Before he could come to grips with that, he was killed. In a sense, the dream killed him. If he had grasped a different dream..."

"You think I've latched onto the wrong dream?"

"Not at all. I'm just suggesting that the Disney reality might not live up to the dream. If it doesn't, you might be disappointed."

"It's okay, Mom. It's like Christmas."

"What do you mean?"

"When I was little, I lived for Christmas. Every year, I got this idea in my head. Everything I wanted would be under the tree. Snow would coat the trees and turn everything white. We'd have a fire and watch a movie and the day would be...perfect. It never worked that way. The gifts that I thought would make me happy did make me happy...for a little while. We rarely had snow on the ground. Everything was gray and dingy. Yet, every year, I dreamed. Disney is like that, isn't it?"

"It's going to be really great, but will it outdo the fantasies inside your head? Maybe not."

"Like Gatsby."

"Exactly."

"That's an important lesson to learn, isn't it?" Cori asked.

Hope said, "It might be like vacation hotels."

"What?"

Hope turned onto their street. "You plan a vacation. You go online and find the perfect hotel, the perfect room. The photos on the website are fantastic, but the hotel never looks like the photos. Oh, the hotel is nice, but it can't match the online perfection. No hotel ever looks better than its website."

Cori chuckled. "That's true. The pictures of food from restaurants are like that, too. In real life, the food doesn't look the same as the photos."

Hope nodded. "Yet, we still go on vacations, we still go to restaurants, and we still dream."

Coir laughed. "Remind me of Gatsby when I don't get what I thought I would."

"You'll remind yourself."

As soon as they parked in their driveway, Cori left to see Lottie and Hope went up to the attic office where Hercule-Max plinked away at his keyboard. Bijou rested next to him all curled up on a blanket.

"Are the little gray cells working?" Hope asked.

"They are, but, at the moment, they are not working all that well. I have begun to research writer's block."

"That's somewhat common with authors. I'm sure you'll work through it."

"I hope so. My brain feels overtaxed. I'm not sure I have the capacity for a murder mystery."

"Keep plugging away. A good story isn't written before lunch."

"I read where some writer said the world is filled with would-be authors who don't know what to do with a rainy Sunday afternoon."

"There you go. Of course, some writers will hire a psychologist to help them through the rough patches."

"There are no psychologists who work with ghosts."

Hope laughed. "I wonder why."

"We don't always pay our bills." Max winked.

"Indeed."

Allison was on time which Hope appreciated.

"Coffee?" Hope asked.

"Wine, white wine, if you have some," Allison replied. "It's been a long day."

Hope poured two glasses and handed one to Allison who was already seated at the kitchen table. Bijou sat near the woman's chair staring at her.

"Is your daughter home?" Allison asked.

"No, she's at a friend's house. Why?"

"I wanted to congratulate her. She did get a role in a Disney production, right?"

"She hasn't started yet, but, yes, she's been offered a contract."

"Terrific. You know, I wanted to be an actress when I was growing up. I thought that would be the coolest thing. In high school and college, I starred in all the plays. I thought I was pretty good. No, I was pretty good."

"What happened? Why did you opt for psychology?"

"Backup. I wanted a backup plan. My mother

used to tell me not to put all my eggs in one basket. She wanted me to have more than one dream."

"That's a good strategy."

"It is if you aren't good enough."

"You weren't good enough?" Hope asked.

"I was, and I wasn't. That's not quite right. I was a good actor, but I didn't look good enough. I shouldn't tell you this, but I've had more than my share of cosmetic surgery. Boobs, tummy, nose, lips. I went to the best I can be."

"You're an attractive woman," Hope assured her.

Allison finished her glass, and Hope poured her another.

"Attractive is what they call you when you're not beautiful. I wanted to be beautiful. It didn't work. My … energy didn't make it to film. I didn't have audience appeal, whatever that is. So, I passed on that dream and started helping other women whose looks didn't coincide with their wishes."

"I think we all wish we looked a little better."

"That's what I told Szymon. He thought his nose was too big."

"When did you tell him that?"

"The last time I saw him, right before he…" Her voice trailed off.

Hope studied Allison, noting that her large eyes had narrowed a little.

"Before he died?" Hope asked. "What else did you argue about?"

Allison sat up straight. "I don't know what you're talking about."

Hope played her hunch. "Rowdy Sherman saw you with Szymon the night he died. He said you were arguing."

"Oh, you can't believe what Rowdy tells you. He might have killed Gerald, you know."

"Come on, Allison, you can tell me. Pamela is already in jail for the murder. What were you discussing with Szymon? By the way, how did you know his name was Szymon?"

"He told me, I think. I don't remember. I'm not sure we even talked that night."

"You did. You were overheard. Want to know what I think? I think he knew you were stealing from the partnership. Did he guess that you killed Gerald, or did he know?"

"What are you talking about?" Allison's voice sounded high-pitched.

"Next question. Did Pamela tell you her password for the payment system, or did you manage to steal it?"

Allison laughed, a fake laugh. Hope suddenly understood why she never made it as an actress.

"I heard you were a great detective, not someone mentally challenged," Allison said.

"Let me lay it out for you. You were stealing from the partnership. I'm guessing you needed money for your lifestyle and maybe for more cosmetic surgeries. You used Pamela's ID, so she would look like the thief. Gerald found the thefts and did some investigating. He soon learned the truth. That's when you decided to kill him. You had no trouble getting fentanyl from your patients who were addicted to the drug. Then, you waited. Gerald died, and you're not a suspect. Then, Szymon figured out the scam and started blackmailing you. He was greedy, and you couldn't allow him to bleed you dry. So, you killed him and framed Pamela."

Allison shook her head in disbelief. "What an imagination you have. You should be a novelist."

"You do know the police will discover the truth when they deep dive into your whereabouts at the time of Szymon's murder. They'll find the users who gave you the pills for disposal. They'll trace down the money you stole and where it went. Your financials will give you away. I might suggest that you work out some kind of source for the extra money you spend, perhaps a dead uncle or something."

Allison's smile flickered for a moment. For Hope, it was proof. Allison would soon be behind bars.

"In movies, I would now confess," Allison said, "but this isn't a movie."

"You can maintain your innocence. That's to be expected, but the evidence will send you to prison."

"You play poker?"

Hope shook her head. "I'm not good at cards."

"There's an old expression… 'in for a dime, in for a dollar.' It means you keep doing what you're doing." Allison reached into her purse and pulled out a small revolver. "Let's take a ride."

20

———

Hope looked straight into Allison's eyes. "I don't think so."

"Why not?"

"Because I made sure Detective Robinson knew you were coming. You won't get away with it."

Allison frowned. "That adds a level of complication, but it hardly saves you. In fact, it makes it easier in some respects. I don't have to get away with anything. I shoot you, wipe the gun clean, and drop it in the backyard. When questioned, I say I found you dead. Who would suspect me? I have no reason to kill you."

"It won't fly, Allison. Two wine glasses, GSR on your hand and clothes. You don't stand a chance against modern forensics."

"You're helping me, I hope you realize that."

"You won't be able to improvise your way out of this," Hope pointed out.

"I can't let you live. You must see that."

"You can't get away with another murder. I hope you can see that."

"It's not insurmountable. I simply have to think for a moment, and I'm pretty sure the solution is as near as your bedroom."

"My bedroom? You're not thinking well. Must be the wine."

"Up you go, Hope. Let's take a walk."

Hope didn't move.

"If you force me to tie you up, then I'll do that. Of course, that's after I bludgeon you with the gun. I'd hate to do that. Your daughter would be so upset when she found you."

"You're thinking of my daughter's feelings now?" Hope stood.

"I don't enjoy hurting people. I'm a psychologist. I live to help, not harm."

"Two murders about to become three pretty much negate your 'I'm-here-to-help' stance."

"I didn't want to kill anyone. Oh, Gerald deserved it. All he had to do was let me pay the money back, but no, he couldn't do that. He wanted to put me in prison. That's insane. I didn't deserve that." Allison waved the pistol. "Start walking."

"You won't be able to sleep at night."

Allison laughed. "Oh my, that's a good one. I've studied the mind and its dreams. People get over everything. In time, I will have replaced all the bad scenes with new ones. I doubt if I'll remember if your eyes were blue or green."

"A few rough nights and you're in the clear?"

"There will be some anxiety, I'm sure, but I can handle that. There are drugs for it. Besides, I'll move as soon as I can. Out of sight, out of mind. You know those old sayings really do mean something."

"A guilty conscience is heavier than an anchor."

"Is that a real saying?"

"I just made it up."

Allison laughed. "That's a good one. I'll use it in my sessions."

Hope led the way to her bedroom.

"Sit on the floor," Allison said and backed toward the closet. "You see what I'm doing, Hope. I'm going to use your clothes to cover mine. That way there will be no gunpowder residue on me. A hat, gloves, coat, shoes. The police will have a devil of a time figuring out why there is GSR on your clothes. Of course, they probably won't even test anything. It doesn't matter. I'll be safe."

Hope watched as Allison slipped on a long trench coat, rather ugly hat, and some gloves she found. Hope's shoes were a size too large, but that hardly mattered. In a minute, Allison looked like she was heading out into a storm.

"Not exactly fashionable, is it?"

"Ask the man behind you," Hope said.

"Please, Hope, from you? That's the oldest play in the book. There is no one behind me. We're quite alone. Now close your eyes."

"Why?"

"I don't want to see them when I shoot you."

"You're not going to shoot me," Hope told the woman.

"Why not?"

"Because you're about to get beaned by a rather thick book."

Allison chuckled. "Right to the end. Well done."

Hope watched as Max slammed the book into the back of Allison's head. Hair and hat cushioned the blow, but Allison still staggered. Hope was off the floor in a flash as Max hammered Allison a second time. She collapsed, stunned. Hope grabbed the pistol.

"Thank you," she told the ghost.

"My pleasure." Max smiled and bowed, and then he disappeared.

On the hardwood floor, Allison moaned.

21

Hope stood behind the cameras and watched. In front of her was the set, which was an ice cream shop. Bright colors, photos of cones, sundaes, and banana splits, tile floor, ordinary tables and chairs ... it was the stuff of small-town squares in the middle of summer. Cori, in a crisp yellow uniform, stood behind the counter ready to serve the boy on the other side. In a few seconds, they would both burst into song, a song Cori had just learned.

Hope moved slightly in order to get a better view. The camera operator and director were in front of her.

As she waited, she considered what had happened to Allison and her story about being clubbed from behind. Hope's version of the attack was far different from Allison's. Detective Robinson believed Hope. Allison was going to prison for many years, perhaps for the rest of her life. That's what happens to murderers.

On cue, the cameras came alive.

The boy sang.

Cori sang.

And Hope just stared at her daughter performing and smiled. *Dreams do come true.*

THANK YOU FOR READING!

Books by J.A. Whiting can be found here:
amazon.com/author/jawhiting

To hear about new books and book sales, please sign up for our mailing list at:
jawhiting.com

Your email will never be sold, shared, or spammed.

If you enjoyed the book, please consider leaving a review. A few words are all that's needed. It would be very much appreciated.

BOOKS BY J.A. WHITING & NELL MCCARTHY

HOPE HERRING PARANORMAL COZY MYSTERIES

TIPPERARY CARRIAGE COMPANY COZY MYSTERIES

BOOKS BY J. A. WHITING

SWEET COVE PARANORMAL COZY MYSTERIES

LIN COFFIN PARANORMAL COZY MYSTERIES

CLAIRE ROLLINS PARANORMAL COZY MYSTERIES

MURDER POSSE PARANORMAL COZY MYSTERIES

PAXTON PARK PARANORMAL COZY MYSTERIES

ELLA DANIELS WITCH COZY MYSTERIES

SEEING COLORS PARANORMAL COZY MYSTERIES

OLIVIA MILLER MYSTERIES (not cozy)

SWEET ROMANCES by JENA WINTER

COZY BOX SETS

BOOKS BY J.A. WHITING & ARIEL SLICK

GOOD HARBOR WITCHES PARANORMAL COZY MYSTERIES

BOOKS BY J.A. WHITING & AMANDA DIAMOND

PEACHTREE POINT COZY MYSTERIES

DIGGING UP SECRETS PARANORMAL COZY
MYSTERIES

BOOKS BY J.A. WHITING & MAY STENMARK

MAGICAL SLEUTH PARANORMAL WOMEN'S FICTION COZY MYSTERIES

HALF MOON PARANORMAL MYSTERIES

VISIT US

jawhiting.com

bookbub.com/authors/j-a-whiting

amazon.com/author/jawhiting

facebook.com/jawhitingauthor

bingebooks.com/author/ja-whiting

Made in United States
North Haven, CT
11 November 2024

60161121R00152